FLiRT

High Fashion

By Nicole Clarke

GROSSET & DUNLAP
Published by the Penguin Group
Penguin Group (USA) Inc., 375 Hudson Street,
New York, New York 10014, U.S.A.
Penguin Group (Canada), 90 Eglinton Avenue East, Suite
700, Toronto, Ontario, Canada M4P 2Y3
(a division of Pearson Penguin Canada Inc.)
Penguin Books Ltd, 80 Strand, London WC2R 0RL, England
Penguin Ireland, 25 St Stephen's Green, Dublin 2, Ireland
(a division of Penguin Books Ltd)
Penguin Group (Australia), 250 Camberwell Road,
Camberwell, Victoria 3124, Australia
(a division of Pearson Australia Group Pty Ltd)
Penguin Books India Pvt Ltd, 11 Community
Centre, Panchsheel Park, New Delhi - 110 017, India
Penguin Group (NZ), Cnr Airborne and Rosedale Roads,
Albany, Auckland 1310, New Zealand
(a division of Pearson New Zealand Ltd)
Penguin Books (South Africa) (Pty) Ltd, 24 Sturdee
Avenue, Rosebank, Johannesburg 2196, South Africa

Penguin Books Ltd, Registered Offices:
80 Strand, London WC2R 0RL, England

Cover and interior design by Michelle Martinez Design, Inc.
Illustrations by Marilena Perilli.

Library of Congress Control Number: 2005036624

ISBN 0-448-44122-5   10 9 8 7 6 5 4 3 2 1

FLiRT
High Fashion

By Nicole Clarke

Grosset & Dunlap

chapter one

"**O**livia, are you listening to me?"

"Pardon? Oh, of course, Demetria."

Olivia Bourne-Cecil looked up from her desk at *Flirt* magazine, where she was interning for the summer in the fashion department. Her mentor at the magazine, Fashion Editor Demetria Tish, was a former supermodel and all-around expert in all things couture-related. She was also, it seemed, not exactly Olivia's biggest fan. At present, she was peering down at Olivia as though the sixteen-year-old girl were something she had accidentally stepped in on the way to work. And a not-very-pleasant something, at that.

Demetria herself reported to Josephine Bishop, the CEO, publisher, and editor-in-chief of *Flirt* and the vast multi-media empire that it spanned. Ms. Bishop was notoriously hard on herself and her staff, which could explain the mild resentment that Olivia felt radiating off of Demetria and onto herself. Olivia's

At present, she was peering down at Olivia as though the sixteen-year-old girl were something she had accidentally stepped in on the way to work.

parents were old friends of Ms. Bishop's and, therefore, Olivia tended to be one of the few staff members—however temporarily so—to escape the mogul's rather consistent wrath.

"We'll be having our weekly staff meeting on Monday, and Bishop will be expecting us to present a concept for the fall issue," Demetria said. "And since each of the interns is given the opportunity to compose a piece on their area of expertise, this will most likely be your chance. You'll want to be ready. Give it some thought over the weekend."

Olivia had other plans for "over the weekend." Brooklyn plans. She couldn't believe it, and yet, there it was: Kiyoko Katsuda, another *Flirt* intern, had gotten a lead on a loft party that she wanted them to go to that night.

"It's Friday," Kiyoko had said, over a breakfast of curbside bagels. "And I'm telling you, this girl knew my sister, Miko, back in university. The party is going to be totally off the hook."

Olivia had had her doubts—she'd never been to the outer boroughs of New York City, after all—but she had kept them to herself. She didn't want to be the wet blanket among her other, flirtier friends, all of whom seemed wildly independent.

For now, though, Olivia merely glanced up at Demetria. "Haute and heavy," she said. It was a tagline she'd been toying with for about a week or so now, knowing as she did that she was bound to get called to task sooner rather than later.

There was that look again, that "do I smell something?" look. "Come again?" Demetria asked.

"Haute and heavy," Olivia repeated, a touch less confidently this time around. "A return to high fashion." She shrugged, reading absolutely zero enthusiasm in Demetria's deadpan expression. "I can work on it."

"See that you do," Demetria suggested brightly. "You've got the weekend."

She shuffled off, her sky-high stilettos leaving a trail in the carpet beneath her.

Before Olivia could catch her breath, someone else was bearing over her. This time it was Kiyoko herself, tapping her fuchsia Hello Kitty watch impatiently. "The girls are already downstairs, lad," she said. "Get yourself together, hey?"

⊚　　⊚　　⊚　　⊚

Getting herself together proved easier said than done, Olivia soon realized. Once back at the *Flirt* intern loft in SoHo, the girls quickly scarfed down pizza, then ran back to their respective rooms to change for the party. It was then that Olivia first encountered the problem that she was facing.

> **But what did one wear to a party in Williamsburg? She had no idea. She wasn't even completely sure where Williamsburg was, after all.**

As a member of London high society, Olivia was impeccably mannered, well-groomed, and always prim and proper. She had the perfect ensemble for a garden party or a coming-out ball. But what did one wear to a party in Williamsburg? She had no idea. She wasn't even completely sure where Williamsburg was, after all.

"It's hopeless," she said, turning to face Melanie Henderson, who had taken all of three seconds to get ready for the party and now sat on Olivia's bed, surveying Liv's vast wardrobe with considerable sympathetic concern. "I've nothing that would work."

"You're being silly. It doesn't matter what you wear," Mel said. Easy for Mel to say; the girl was fearless and, also, somewhat clueless. She absolutely never cared what people thought of her and usually was blissfully oblivious. For the most part, her genuine warmth and sincerity was met with what Mel herself referred to as "good karma." When she'd arrived in New York and had to prove herself to Bishop, it had been one of the few challenging interpersonal situations she'd ever had to navigate.

Liv leveled Mel with a raised eyebrow.

"You can borrow something of mine," Mel offered brightly. "I know you won't, but you can."

Liv shook her head no. Mel was the original hippie chick who almost always wandered around looking like a long-lost cousin of the Olsen twins. A particularly stunning cousin, to be sure, but nonetheless . . . right now, for instance, she was wearing frayed, faded jeans and a teeny-tiny tank top. As a concession to the festive occasion, she had broken out her "fancy" flip-flops, a pink pair embellished with sequins. "Your clothes wouldn't work for me," Liv said. "I don't reckon we're even the same size, anyway." She sighed and blew the tips of her fringe out of her eyes.

"You're being ridiculous," Mel said, popping up from the bed and crossing the room so she stood, alongside Olivia, in front of the open wardrobe doors. She began to determinedly flip through the hangers. "Seriously, girl? If between the two of us, with all of the clothes that you've brought with you, we can't pick an outfit? That would be a sad, sad, state of affairs." She stopped at a black cashmere sweater set. "What about this?"

Olivia gave a sharp nod of her head no. "Too matronly, don't you think?"

Melanie smiled knowingly. "The problem with you, London, is that you never use your imagination."

◕   ◕   ◕   ◕

Half an hour later Olivia stood in her bedroom, the tank from her sweater set and a denim skirt hanging from her frame in all the right places. Alexa Veron had talked her into a pair of red sandals, and Kiyoko had flipped the edges of her bob out with a straightening iron. She looked . . . well, she looked adorable, she had to admit. Like herself, but with the slightest hint of an edge. It was perfect.

"Are we ready to roll, lads?" Kiyoko asked.

All four girls nodded in unison.

As ready as I'll ever be, Olivia thought. *That's for sure.*

◕   ◕   ◕   ◕

Now, Olivia Bourne-Cecil knew how to party. Born and bred (no pun intended) in a several-million-dollar mansion set just back off of the Hampstead Heath, Olivia had been acting as the hostess with . . . well, with rather quite a lot, since essentially the age when she first learned to walk. She knew the proper place setting for a seven-course meal, she could tell you which plates one used for finger sandwiches (it was a platter, and not plates at all, in the end). When her father's good friend Nigel Drake had been knighted by the Queen, she'd worn a Vera Wang gown worth as much as an inexpensive car. Not to the knighting, of course; that would have been, all in all, a bit *much*. But at the ball afterward, Olivia had dazzled in a shimmer of taffeta and lace.

She'd emceed junior auctions and announced at the annual Marks and Spencer fashion show. At the event, she'd hand-selected some of the fashions as her mother Eleanor Bourne-Cecil's right hand. Her mother had even trusted her with the menu-planning and floral arrangements for some of the Bourne-Cecils' smaller garden soirees.

So, yes, when it came to social functions, Olivia was certainly as gracious, poised, and polished as the next girl. More so, even, than most. But that was back in England, back in Hampstead, back in London, where she and her family were part of a society so elite, she was just shy of royalty.

In other words, a right far cry from Williamsburg, Brooklyn.

Williamsburg, Brooklyn, was for all intents and purposes a foreign country to Olivia.

"What's our stop, then?" Olivia asked, clutching the subway pole and struggling to keep her balance in her lovely sandals.

"Bedford Avenue," Kiyoko said. She squinted at the subway map that hung in the car. "We have two more stops to go."

They were riding the L train, one of the few subways that ran both across Manhattan and into Brooklyn. It was, however, much like all the other subway cars that Olivia had ever ridden in: dirty, sticky, and poorly ventilated. Not that the tube back home was so much more glamorous.

"Bedford Avenue—that's where all the shops are and stuff." It was Ben, Alexa's brand-new boyfriend, who had joined them for the party. They'd only recently gotten together, and Olivia didn't blame Alexa for wanting to show him off at the weekend. Ben was very cute and very worthy of showing off. Alexa was chuffed to have him at her side, that much was obvious.

"Yeah, but the loft is a little bit of a walk from the main drag," Kiyoko warned them. She shrugged noncommittally.

"Keeks? Define *little bit of a walk*," Mel said, a perky smile plastered on her face. Mel was one of the only girls in the loft who could get away with giving Kiyoko a hard time. Which she did, when she needed to.

For now, however, Kiyoko only shook her head a brief but definitive no. "It's all good," she said. "You'll see."

◉   ◉   ◉   ◉

When they reached their stop, Ben and the girls moved through the turnstiles and headed up the stairs. From there, they walked down streets that morphed from funky and boutique-lined to borderline desolate and industrial. Ben pointed out a bookstore that he and his friends liked, and a bar that the postcollegiate hipsters enjoyed.

Finally, they made it to the building where the party was being held. It was an old warehouse that someone had had the presence of mind to gut renovate for a young, increasingly gentrified artist community. (This was the trend in New York City, Liv knew. Her parents were, in addition to their various other pursuits, deep into real estate.) The group rode in an old refurbished freight elevator that closed by hand with an iron gate. When the gate opened again, they found themselves deposited directly into the loft's main living area.

Interesting, Olivia thought as she looked around. The loft was exactly as overwhelming as she had imagined. Dizzying, in a way that she might have found exhilarating if it weren't for the complete sensory overload. Three sides of the large room were covered by waist-level walls of thick, translucent glass. Beyond the glass toward the back was a kitchen area offset by a stainless steel island on rolling casters. The "bedroom" was off to the right. At least Liv *thought* it was the bedroom—all she could see was some furniture and a strategically placed Chinese screen. The primary sources of light were clusters of tiny votives set on sconces along the walls, though the walls were floor-to-ceiling windows.

> ## "The floors were painted brick red."

The floors were painted brick red.

Kiyoko introduced Ben and the girls to the hostesses, a sculptress and a poet: "Lads, this is Sonia and Beth, yeah?" As though they were one person.

Sonia was an old friend of Kiyoko's older sister, a model who was spending her summer in London. Sonia was astonishingly petite, boneless, ethereal, and perfectly at home in this otherworldly setting. Her hair, a close pixie cut a la Twiggy in her heyday, was so blond, it was almost white, and her eyes were a piercing, electric blue. Olivia instantly adored Sonia and her effortless mix of nonchalance and intensity.

Sonia gestured toward the kitchen, explaining about the food and drink ("beer and mixers in the fridge; wine and hard stuff on the counter"), and told the girls to "like, make yourselves at home."

"Did you refurbish this flat yourself?" Olivia asked, frankly curious and also impressed.

Sonia nodded. "Well, not with my bare hands, but sure. The artistic vision was mine."

"And mine!" Beth insisted, poking Sonia in the ribs. Both girls giggled.

Sonia waved at an enormous stereo system looming in the far corner. "Did you BYO iPods?" The premise of the party was that people could hook their iPods up to the stereo and share their music. Which had been a huge draw for Kiyoko, who was practically defined by her musical taste.

Kiyoko grinned. "You had to ask?" She waggled her eyebrows at her friends. "I'll be your guest DJ for the night. You know where to find me." And off she floated, enormous, oversize earrings swinging against her shoulders and sky-high platforms thudding. She'd been at the party for all of three seconds, Liv mused, and she already well owned the joint. Probably thought that guy over by the stereo with her—the one with the shaved head and tattooed forearms fiddling with the speakers— wanted her. He probably *did* want her. Poor fool. Kiyoko had a boyfriend and, besides that, had a tendency to flirt inconsequentially with nearly every boy she met. Who all had a tendency not to mind that much.

Alexa, meanwhile, danced, enjoying Ben's company and attention. Alexa had met Ben in one of those classic New York City stories, the kind of thing that only happened in films. That is, he waited on her every morning at the local coffee shop, finally mustering up the nerve to ask her on an actual date.

Olivia had been on plenty of dates with some of the most eligible young men in England (again, just shy

> **She knew how to be interesting, animated, and charming with a member of the opposite sex, but she had not a clue what that scary/wonderful rush to the stomach that Alexa was always describing actually felt like. Unfortunately.**

of royalty). But she'd never properly fancied a boy or gone out with one on a date that hadn't been organized and heartily endorsed by her parents. She knew how to be interesting, animated, and charming with a member of the opposite sex, but she had not a clue what that scary/wonderful rush to the stomach that Alexa was always describing actually felt like. Unfortunately.

Mel was lounging languidly on a sofa, oversize plastic cup in her hand and a perma-grin affixed to her lovely, all-American features. She was laughing openly at something someone else on the sofa was saying, and for what felt the umpteenth time, Olivia envied Mel's ease with strangers and strange situations. Liv could navigate social situations certainly, but Mel seemed to quite genuinely enjoy them. Baffling.

As for herself, Liv was leaning up against a wall in

one of the only places where the wood-to-glass ratio was high enough so as not to give her vertigo. She surveyed the scene. She was one of the few people in the room whose only visible piercings were in her actual earlobes, and her outfit, while cute enough, was not going to get her a spot in any "Top Ten Trendy Teens" list anytime soon.

Right, well, good thing they're all too busy enjoying the party to take notice of my outfit. Good thing, indeed.

She couldn't help it—she was bored, if only a bit. She glanced down into her own plastic cup. Empty, diet soda remnants sludged along the bottom of the cup unappealingly. She needed a prop. That meant refilling the cup.

Off to the kitchen, then.

There, she found mostly an assortment of empty bottles: wine bottles, beer bottles, and a huge bottle of something that looked quite a bit like hard alcohol. Sonia's little tutorial had all but slipped from Liv's memory. No matter. While underage drinking in London was far less taboo than here in New York City, it wasn't at all what Liv was interested in just now. She'd discovered, upon abandoning her post in the living "room," that she was thirsty. A glass of water would be perfect.

The problem was, there didn't seem to be any water to be found in the kitchen. A tall freestanding cooler proved, disappointingly, to be empty, as were all of the large plastic bottles resting on the counter next to the refrigerator. What now?

"Tap water's probably safe."

Liv whirled around, wondering where the unsolicited—but entirely welcome—advice had come from.

And stopped in her tracks.

The boy was either in his late teens or early twenties. He wore duo-toned neutral-colored Pumas that were smarter than regular trainers, and tan corduroys that were worn in at the knees and lived-in-looking. He had on a short-sleeved button-down shirt, untucked, and over that a sweater vest that Olivia was certain was vintage. Classic. His skin was smooth and darkly tanned, and his eyes were massive. His hair was cut close to the scalp. He smiled, and his teeth were blindingly white. He was fit—she could tell, even through the layers of shirt/vest—and he was gorgeous. He was absolutely the best-looking boy Olivia had ever seen in real life, undoubtedly.

She dropped her cup.

The plastic made a soft skittering sound against the floor, startling Liv back to reality momentarily. "Right," she said, bending at the waist and retrieving it. "Pardon?"

"The tap." He smiled again and pointed at the sink, another stainless steel contraption that was as sleek as any installation Liv had ever seen at the Tate

Modern. He shrugged. "You looked thirsty."

"Quite right," Liv agreed, feeling her cheeks fill with color. How embarrassing, to lose control entirely at first sight of a proper—what was it that Mel called them?—*hottie*. "The tap." She crossed over to the sink and quickly refilled her cup. Now she had a cupful of soda backwash and tepid, rusty, New York City water. Unappealing. But the boy was watching her—now with a look of curious bemusement—so she lifted the cup to her lips and sipped gingerly, trying not to wince. "Lovely."

He burst out laughing. "I'll bet. Here's a hint." He leaned in. "Poker? Not your game."

"Am I that transparent?"

"Don't worry—it's endearing. You don't have that glazed gaze of ironic detachment that's, you know, the calling card of most young New Yorkers."

"Well, technically, I'm a Londoner," Liv pointed out.

"Also endearing. I love the accent. Though you must get that a lot."

"Sometimes," Liv admitted. "I suppose I'm a novelty."

"I'll bet," the boy said. He stuck out his hand to shake. "I'm Eli. Sonia is my TA at NYU."

"You sculpt?" Liv asked, instantly impressed. Or rather, more impressed.

"I try," he corrected her. "I'm actually a film student, but I need a fine arts credit, and the professor for the class has an amazing reputation. He does mostly large-scale, abstract installations like Christo and stuff. Did you see 'The Gates' last winter in Central Park?"

He thought she lived in New York, full-time. Maybe he thought she was in college. That was brilliant. But she couldn't lie. She was rubbish at telling lies. "No, actually, I'm just in town for summer holiday," Liv said. "I have an internship at *Flirt* magazine. Have you heard of it?"

"Sure," he said, impressing Liv all over again. She didn't expect a boy to be reading fashion magazines on any sort of regular basis. "That's cool. *You're* cool."

"She's cool, she's hot, she's bloody all-temperature," Kiyoko agreed, striding into the kitchen and helping herself to a Red Bull from the refrigerator. She cracked the can, swigged, swallowed, and pressed the cold aluminum against her forehead. "It's crazy crowded here, lads," she said. "Eli, long time no see."

"Hey, Kiyoko. I didn't know you were in town."

"Interning at *Flirt*. I got the entertainment beat."

"That sounds about right."

"Yeah, well. I wanted fashion," she said with a brief glance in Liv's direction, and not an entirely friendly one, at that. "But you know. Things happen."

Liv knew that Kiyoko had been disappointed

that she'd gotten the internship in the entertainment department while Liv had been assigned to fashion. But they really hadn't had very much say in their assignments, and anyway, Liv just couldn't bring herself to be disappointed that things had worked out the way she'd wanted them to. She was as entitled to the fashion beat as anyone, wasn't she? Her own personal style was certainly more . . . *understated* than Kiyoko's, but it was impeccable. That much she knew. Anyhow, most of the time she and Kiyoko got on just fine—especially when Mel was around to mediate—but every now and then, tension reared its ugly head. Like now, for instance. Maybe Kiyoko was just feeling territorial about Liv sharing her toys . . . or rather, her friends?

"Whatever," Eli said. "I'm sure you'll teach the editors a little something about music."

Kiyoko smirked. "If they're lucky." She looked again at Olivia, this time questioningly. "She behaving herself? Playing nice?"

"She's playing ultranice," Eli confirmed. "You missed it. I was just introducing her to the wonders of New York City tap water."

" Maybe Kiyoko was just feeling territorial about Liv sharing her toys . . . or rather, her friends? "

> **"** *Olivia suddenly found herself wishing the ground would open up and consume her whole.* **"**

"Tap water? Horrors!" Kiyoko mimicked. Liv wasn't sure how good-naturedly the teasing was intended, so she chose to ignore it. What else was there to do?

"London here isn't too familiar with parties that don't appear in the society pages," Kiyoko joked. Again, Liv ignored the semibarb.

"Yeah, it's obvious that she's high class," Eli replied, in a tone that was far more complimentary than Kiyoko's had been.

Kiyoko's smile stretched a tad too tightly across her lips, like she'd maybe swallowed something down the wrong pipe but didn't want to embarrass herself. Olivia suddenly found herself wishing the ground would open up and consume her whole.

Before it could, though, Mel wandered over brightly. "Liv! Kiyoko! There you are." She glanced to the right and left furtively. "I need your help."

"What's the what, lad?" Kiyoko asked eagerly.

Mel shrugged. "That guy over there—" She pointed. "I think his name is Chad."

"Todd," Kiyoko corrected, causing Olivia to

marvel once more. *How* was it that the girl knew literally every single person in New York City?

"Right. Anyway . . ." Mel grimaced. "We were talking, and I *swear* I was just trying to be nice, but . . ."

Kiyoko rolled her eyes. "Let me guess. He wants to marry you and have a million of your babies. Jeez, girl, you're a hazard to the male population."

"You don't seem to know your own strength," Olivia agreed.

"It's not on purpose," Mel said, shaking her head ruefully. That much was true. Mel was good-natured, kind-hearted, trusting, and open. She'd never deliberately try to lead a boy on, though her wide-eyed enthusiasm had backfired and sent the wrong message on more than one occasion. "Anyway, the point is that I think I need to get out of here, fast. He's got that deer-in-headlights expression and I feel too guilty. Besides"—she waved her wrist at her roommates—"curfew in, like, twenty minutes."

"Curfew, please," Kiyoko snorted. "I've got at least six more playlists cued up, and I'm sure Emma went to bed hours ago." She was referring to their housemother, Emma Lyric, who was young and friendly but not entirely without authority. If they were to get caught sneaking in past curfew, Emma would not be thrilled. But that didn't seem to bother Kiyoko.

"Yeah, Alexa had pretty much the same reaction

when I suggested that we *vamanos.* I think she and Ben are, uh, occupied." Mel was too delicate to say more on the matter, but the girls could guess what she meant.

Olivia gulped down the remains of her metallic-tinged tap water and tossed her cup into the large plastic garbage bag that sat on the floor next to the refrigerator. Thankfully, it went in—she wasn't keen on getting any closer to the sticky trash than was absolutely necessary. "I'm not bothered leaving now, Mel, really," she said. "I'm tired. I'll go home with you."

"Great," Mel said immediately. "We can leave together—if you and Alexa look out for each other, Keeks." She looked at Kiyoko meaningfully. *Among other things,* Olivia mused, *Mel is the only girl who can get away with calling Kiyoko "Keeks."*

"Surely," Kiyoko agreed.

"*Please* don't be too late past curfew," Mel continued imploringly. "It kicks my chakras all out of alignment when I have to stress over you."

"How many times do I have to tell you, lad? You have to own your own chakras," Kiyoko said. "They can't be on *my* shoulders. But your concern is duly noted."

> **"How many times do I have to tell you, lad? You have to own your own chakras. "**

"We'd better be getting on," Olivia said. "I don't know about chakras, auras, or any of that, but I don't fancy giving Emma a reason to be upset with us."

"Was it something I said?" Eli joked.

Olivia found herself blushing all over again. Clearly, Eli had that effect on her. "Of course not. It was lovely to meet you, Eli," she said, wishing but not actually allowing herself to hope that he would take her mobile number.

"Lovely to meet you, too," he said, doing his best British accent. It wasn't all that bad, Olivia noted with glee. "But there's just one thing."

"What's that?" she asked, grinning like a lunatic completely involuntarily.

"You still haven't told me your name."

She hadn't, she realized. Prim and proper Olivia Bourne-Cecil had fallen short on one of the most basic tenets of good etiquette.

Thankfully, the situation was easily rectified. And then it truly was time to leave.

⊙　　⊙　　⊙　　⊙

It was only eleven thirty on a Friday night, but residential Williamsburg felt deserted as Mel and Liv made their way to the subway. Liv supposed that most of the young hipsters had made their way to the bars and clubs by now. They wouldn't be back much before the first edges of dawn began to uncurl.

"So," Mel began casually. "Eli."

Olivia raised an eyebrow at her friend. "Eli, what?"

"Eli, *cute*," Mel said emphatically.

"He is, isn't he?" Liv agreed, giggling. "For an American." She tried to be cool and aloof, to squelch the giddy butterflies in her stomach.

> **You've got post-hottie glow.**

"Please," Mel said. "I see right through you. You're glowing. You've got post-hottie glow."

"I suppose so," Olivia sighed wistfully. Eli hadn't taken her number, though, so it looked like post-hottie glow would be the beginning and the end of it. Sad, that. *Poof.* The butterflies were gone—all on their own, all at once.

"Man!" Mel exclaimed, breaking into Olivia's reverie. "Ugh, this is perfect." She rattled around in her oversize bag. "I can't find my MetroCard."

"You had it on the subway ride over here," Liv pointed out.

"Yes, I know," Mel said. "And yet . . ." She wasn't especially upset, just matter-of-fact. Scatterbrained Mel was accustomed to misplacing things. Somehow, whatever she lost always turned up in the end. Things had a way of working out for Mel; she was just lucky, it seemed.

"Well . . ." Olivia scanned the empty streets. "Right there." She indicated a yellow cab making its way down the street. "I swear, you've got some sort of guardian angel looking after you, Melanie. Obviously, that cabbie just dropped off a fare from Manhattan." Out in Brooklyn, Liv knew, if you wanted a cab, you had to call for one in advance.

"Funny," Mel replied. "My guardian angel doesn't much concern himself with my finances. I'm broke. Can't be cabbing it all over town, Liv." She frowned. "Besides, I can always just buy another card."

"Don't be silly," Liv said. "I have plenty of cash. And it's nearly curfew. Let's just take the cab. It'll be much easier. I'm not bothered by paying."

"I know you're not," Mel argued. "But I hate feeling like a charity case."

"That's ridiculous," Liv said. "It's only a few dollars; it's certainly no big deal. Besides, it's far too late to be taking a subway."

"Ridiculous is the idea that eleven thirty on a Friday night is too late to take the subway, but whatever," Mel said. "There's only so many times I'm going to turn down a ride. If you insist."

"I insist," Liv confirmed. "But we'd better run before someone else beats us to it."

෧   ෧   ෧   ෧

The cab ride ended up being less than twenty dollars, even with a tip. *Dead cheap,* Liv thought, *especially compared to the black cabs in London.* She was glad Mel had eventually caved. Olivia respected the fact that her friends didn't want to exploit her for her money, but the truth was, she didn't mind, or rather, didn't feel exploited by it. Why shouldn't they take a cab home when it was convenient and they were running late, anyway?

Unfortunately, Mel had spent the better part of the ride affectionately rehashing the highlights of the evening. Liv was happy to hear her friend talk and glad that Mel had enjoyed herself, but for Liv, Eli was essentially the bright spot of the party. Seeing a new neighborhood and spending time with her friends was lovely, of course, but listening to Mel go on, Liv couldn't help but feel a wistful sort of envy. After tonight, she was more clear than ever: No matter how adept she was at high-society events, she'd never be as comfortable in her own skin as someone like Mel, Kiyoko, or even Alexa was. Those girls were fearless, while Olivia's great talent was knowing how to curtsey (what people didn't

> **" *Olivia's great talent was knowing how to curtsey.* "**

realize was that it mostly had to do with the right kind of skirt).

Knowing how to curtsey got Liv into the gossip pages (where her parents were sure to check up on her comings and goings whilst in the States), but it didn't get her any closer to someone like Eli.

And getting closer to Eli was suddenly a very appealing thought, indeed.

chapter two

"**D**id someone get the plate number of the truck that hit me last night?"

Liv looked up from her reading to see Kiyoko making her way from the bedroom that she shared with Alexa into the common area of the *Flirt* intern loft. The girl had *definitely* seen better mornings. Liv wondered how late Kiyoko and Alexa had stayed out. Thank goodness the two of them roomed together—that made them the perfect partners in crime.

Liv glanced at her antique-set wristwatch: half-eleven. A perfectly respectable time to be up on a Saturday—if one were only first rising. Liv, however, had been in bed—face scrubbed and teeth cleaned rigorously—by one A.M. the night before. And had popped out of bed brightly at nine. She had tried to fall back asleep, but to no avail. Her internal body clock was as fastidious as the rest of her. After thirty minutes of tossing and turning, she finally gave in, grabbed a book, and wandered out to the common area.

" *Her internal body clock was as fastidious as the rest of her.* "

Up on a Saturday morning reading, she thought. *Very sexy. Very glamorous.*

She could tell from the look on Kiyoko's face that her fellow Flirt was thinking the very same thing. "Gosh, lad," she said, yawning loudly, "I guess I should have ordered my wake-up call with you?"

"The light in my bedroom was bright," Liv offered, as though she needed to defend her natural habits. Which, perhaps, she did. Especially with Kiyoko, who seemed to regard manners and propriety as the eighth deadly sin.

"Where's Mel?" Kiyoko asked. Typical. Mel was the common denominator amongst the roommates. What Kiyoko was implying, in essence, was that it was difficult for her to make conversation with Liv all on her own. And maybe it was.

"She went out for a jog. She'll be back soon." *Please,* Olivia prayed internally. She was too tired and a wee bit too self-pitying this morning to deal with Kiyoko by herself.

"A jog? Madness," Kiyoko said. "I do not understand these young girls with their 'health kicks' and 'sound mind, sound body' stuff." She mimicked air

> *I do not understand these young girls with their 'health kicks' and 'sound mind, sound body' stuff.*

quotes with her fingers, sarcasm dripping from the tips of her neon orange manicure.

"Did the *chiquita loca* go running again? *Caramba,* what are we going to do with her?" Alexa asked, bopping into the common room with her ponytail swinging. "She must be stopped."

Olivia had to laugh, despite herself. "She'll be back soon," she said.

"Good, because we're going to brunch," Alexa replied.

"Food? Now you've got my attention," Kiyoko said, crossing her arms and leaning back as though in wait.

"*Sí*, Ben, he recommended a place for me . . . It is in the neighborhood where they . . . 'keep it real'?" She gazed off for a moment, obviously trying to recall whatever it was that she and Ben had discussed when they'd come up for air last night. "The Lower East Side!" She smiled, pleased. "He says there is a jazz brunch down there that is amazing. We should go."

Kiyoko nodded. "Sounds bloody awesome, lad. I'm in. I love a real 'New York neighborhood' experience."

"The Lower East Side, though." The words were out of Olivia's mouth even before she realized she'd been thinking them in her head.

Instantly, Kiyoko bristled. "What?"

"I had read . . . I just meant . . ." Olivia stammered, faltering badly. "Is it safe?" she finished finally, feeling like a right moron. She honestly had no idea. Until this summer, the only time she'd spent in New York City had been with her parents, in places that mostly overlooked Central Park East. Hotel places.

Kiyoko rolled her eyes. "Well, let's see." She made a big show of holding out one hand and ticking off fingers, like a list, as she spoke. "One: There are four of us, so it's not like there are any helpless females just making their way down the street by themselves. Two: It's Saturday morning—not exactly the most crime-ridden, violent hour. Three: Are you kidding? Where were you raised?"

> ❝ *Hampstead, Liv thought. I was raised in Hampstead.* ❞

Hampstead, Liv thought but did not say. *I was raised in Hampstead.*

The truth was, she thought a jazz brunch downtown sounded completely fantastic. And Kiyoko was right—there was no such thing as an unsafe neighborhood in broad daylight when surrounded by friends. She was being silly. And proper. And uptight. As usual. Which was nothing more than a waste of time when one had an entire summer to try things differently. "I would love to come," she heard herself say.

"Perfecto!" Alexa exclaimed, clapping her hands together with glee. "I will shower and get dressed." She dashed off to do just that.

"I will, too," Liv said. "It only takes Mel a moment to sort herself out, and that way we can leave as soon as she gets back." She tucked the book she'd been reading under her arm and wandered off in the same direction as Alexa had gone.

She stopped off in her bedroom to grab her shower caddy. Her roommate, Charlotte Gabel, was all but unconscious in her bed, tangled in a heap of covers. Liv guessed that Charlotte and Gen had been out quite late the night before. Charlotte's bed had been empty when Liv had gone to sleep. They must have sneaked in after curfew.

Liv pulled together her shower things and a towel as quietly as she could. Just as she was on her way out of the room and into the shower, however, she noticed her cell phone sitting on top of her small, spare nightstand: ONE NEW MESSAGE.

She glanced at her watch; anyone she knew in the States would certainly still be sleeping. Which meant that the call was probably from overseas and, in that case, probably from her parents. Which probably wasn't fantastic news. But she had to call them back.

She dialed quickly, hearing the short *bleep* that sounded like an overseas ring. Her mother picked up

> **The call was probably from overseas and, in that case, probably from her parents. Which probably wasn't fantastic news.**

straightaway. "*Olivia*, dear," she trilled. "Did you get my message?"

"No, Mum—er, rather, yes, but I haven't listened to it just yet. I thought it'd be best to phone you first. You know, so I could catch you in person."

"Lovely, darling," her mother said brusquely, suggesting to Liv that she perhaps wasn't really listening to her daughter at all. "Listen, you do remember Lyddie Pearson and her husband, Neil?"

"Yes," Olivia said, searching her brain for the mental image. There it was: Lyddie was tall, thin, and clench-jawed in a manner that recalled Josephine Bishop. She was an art collector . . . whose gallery had recently opened a New York outpost. Liv's heart sank. "Yes, she's just opened the gallery."

"Quite right," her mother said. "And today is the opening."

"A gallery opening on a Saturday morning?" Olivia asked dubiously.

"Well, two in the afternoon is hardly the morning,

dear," her mother countered. "The first private viewing will likely have its own evening affair, but this is just more of a ribbon-cutting sort of thing. Ceremonial, you know."

Liv nodded, then realized that of course her mother couldn't see her over the phone line. "Yes, ceremonial," she said aloud.

"Anyway, the invitation came to us in London— they must have sent it out before they realized that you'd be in New York. Obviously, we won't be able to attend, as Daddy has the museum benefit in Paris tomorrow night. We *would* have flown in . . ."

That wasn't true. They did love New York, and enjoyed jet-setting. But the gallery opening was small enough potatoes that it made more sense to foist the Pearsons off on Liv.

"But someone from our family ought to go, and since you're in the same city, it only makes sense." *There it is.*

"Sensible, right," Liv muttered, more to herself than anyone else. *So much for brunch.* "I wish you had mentioned it sooner," she mumbled.

"What, darling? Don't mutter; I can't make a word out," her mother chastised her.

"I said I'll be glad to go," Olivia said, knowing that it was really the only acceptable reply.

"Brilliant," her mother said. "We do appreciate

> **Lyddie would not recognize me if I walked across the room and snogged her right on the lips.**

this, and Lyddie will be so pleased to see you."

Lyddie would not recognize me if I walked across the room and snogged her right on the lips, Olivia thought but wisely did not say out loud.

Her mother gave her the information for the gallery—somewhere in Chelsea, Olivia noted as she scrawled the address on a scrap of paper—and they said their good-byes. Once off the phone, Olivia collapsed backward onto her bed, sighing heavily. Just a few minutes ago, brunch on the Lower East Side sounded seedy and slightly uncouth. Now that she knew she couldn't go, it sounded like a great, wild, unknown quantity. That she would miss out on. She knew her loftmates—especially Kiyoko—thought she could be a bit frosty. She'd have rather spent the morning proving them wrong. Or at the very least, trying.

She sighed again.

"Jeez, did someone, like, *die* or something?" the mound of bedclothes asked in a muffled voice.

"What? No, of course not." Liv quickly realized that the words were coming from Charlotte. That made

> **"** *Olivia thought Gen was about as shy as she was genuinely sweet— that was to say, not at all.* **"**

a lot more sense than the alternative.

"Then why all the heavy breathing?"

Charlotte and Liv weren't great mates or anything—Charlotte mostly hung on to Genevieve Bishop, who seemed to carry a severe personal grudge against everyone other than Charlotte, at least some of the time. Mel didn't see it—she insisted that Gen was just shy—but Olivia thought Gen was about as shy as she was genuinely sweet—that was to say, not at all.

All things being as they were, Liv didn't feel a great urge to open up to Charlotte. So she simply said, "My plans have gotten a bit mucked up," and left it that. Charlotte didn't reply. Liv turned to look at her, only to find that the lithe, athletic girl had burrowed back underneath her pillow, snoring lightly.

The door to the bedroom creaked open and suddenly Kiyoko was standing over Liv, looking quizzical. "I thought you were going to shower?"

Olivia frowned. "It seems my plans have changed."

ⓖ   ⓖ   ⓖ   ⓖ

"*Olivia*, it's *fantastic* to see you!"

Olivia started backward as Phoebe Winters, an acquaintance from back home, made her way over to say hello. "Did your parents tell you about this show?"

Olivia nodded dumbly. She'd just arrived, and was almost instantly struck speechless by the gallery: smoothly polished wood floors, and waiters circling, offering canapés and mimosas to black-clad art dealers, buyers, and aficionados of all ages.

"Well, I'm glad you're here," Phoebe said, clutching at Olivia's elbow. "There are absolutely *no* cute blokes here. Pity." She giggled.

Olivia flashed back to Eli. She didn't care to meet any cute blokes here. She had already met one. Though, the way she had left things, there was no reason to think he was going to ring her or ask her out.

Pity.

"D'you know, I think I have to visit the loo," Phoebe said, looking suddenly pensive. "Would you mind?" She foisted her mimosa glass off onto Olivia.

"Oh, well, I don't think I'd better—" Olivia began, but Phoebe was already gone. "Sure, why not?" she finished lamely.

From: mtbourne-cecil@runner.uk
To: liv_b-c@flirt.com
Subject: Behaviour unbecoming of a lady

Olivia, dear—

I did happen to see in <u>OK UK</u> a shot of you at the art showing on Saturday. Pleased as I am that you decided to attend the show, I can't help but wonder if perhaps you could have exercised better judgment. I know drinking is taken more lightly in England, but you're in the U.S. now, darling. It's fairly inappropriate for a young lady of merely sixteen years of age to be seen—much less photographed—quaffing champagne, art opening or no.

Surely it was merely an oversight?

Best,
Mum

chapter three

"**O**livia! Staff meeting!"

"Yes, Demetria."

Slowly, Liv pushed her chair backward and picked up the tiny spiral notebook and pencil she used for keeping track of her daily intern tasks. Every Monday morning Josephine Bishop held her staff meeting. She addressed any administrative issues, and then the different departments were called upon to brainstorm and provide feedback. The environment was fairly up and down; it could go from being very collaborative and creative to incredibly cutthroat in a matter of seconds. Olivia was right nervous about how today's meeting would go, as she usually tended to be.

She dutifully followed Demetria into the conference room, a huge space mostly dominated by an enormous glass-topped table. Most of the editors were already gathered, nursing grande cups of designer coffee and semibored expressions. Josephine

" The environment could go from being very collaborative and creative to incredibly cutthroat in a matter of seconds. "

Bishop was settled into her usual seat at the head of the table, her back straight as a pin and her hair, makeup, and outfit practically sprayed on, they were all so stiff.

Magazine publishing was a study in contradictions. Olivia learned this early on in her *Flirt* internship. Josephine Bishop herself, widely considered to be the empress of contemporary fashion media, was a prime example. For one thing, there was her physical presence: impossibly tall and painfully thin. Jet-black hair pulled back so tightly into a bun that it looked painted on. Blood-red lips, all day long—through meetings, phone calls, meals. She exuded restraint, control, and fierce, tense energy from every pore. And yet she was a creative force to be reckoned with, a meat-eating, whiskey-drinking, cigar-smoking woman who could more than hold her own amongst the old boys' network. She was larger than life, which was ironic, given that she probably weighed the equivalent of a high-school student.

> 66 *Magazine publishing was a study in contradictions.* 99

Her staff, too, was composed of brilliant, manic, multitasking geniuses. The magazine ran amid a flurry of shrill cell phones, headsets, mocked-up boards, photo negatives and light boxes, highlighting markers, and bright Post-it flags. Caffeine flowed freely through the halls, and pencils tapped impatiently against desktops. *Flirt* was always shrouded in a thick blanket of high-octane activity.

But none of this was obvious at a Monday morning staff meeting.

Staff meetings were intended to set the tone for the week. Everyone from the editorial departments—that was to say, editorial, art, and production (basically everyone who wasn't on the business side of things)—attended and brainstormed different ideas for upcoming issues. It was less about productivity and more about grandstanding, about face time, Olivia decided. But somehow, things did get done.

Looking around the sparkling glass-and-chrome conference room table now, though, one would never guess that these editors, the sleep-fogged (but dead trendy), spaced-out, can't-believe-it's-Monday-at-ten-already folks, *these* people were responsible for the magazine that, month after month, did no less than set (and reset) the pop culture barometer for most of the western hemisphere.

> **It was less about productivity and more about grandstanding, about face time. But somehow, things did get done.**

As if to punctuate Liv's analysis, Trey Narkisian yawned loudly, not bothering to cover his mouth.

"Are we keeping you up, Trey?" Demetria teased. Again, Olivia had to chalk her mentor's behavior up to basic insecurity: the air had been thick with hints of a corporate reshuffling from which Trey seemed most likely to benefit. Obviously, Demetria was not pleased about this, though Olivia and her friends secretly enjoyed this up-close-and-personal look at corporate machinations.

"Alas, you are," Trey answered. He winked. And yawned again. "But I'll forgive you this time."

"How kind of you, Trey," Bishop said witheringly. "Perhaps we should start with you. Then you can excuse yourself, once you've dazzled us with your stellar contribution." She was kidding, in a very overbearing, scary, rather-not-funny-at-all sort of way. No one left the meeting until it was officially adjourned. And with good reason, too—brainstorming was actually much more productive when there were more people involved. It was chaotic, but true nonetheless.

"Actually, I was hoping we could go first." It was Demetria. Olivia sat straight up. They hadn't discussed going first. Other than their conversation on Friday, she really hadn't been prepped at all.

She couldn't believe that Demetria had swooped in and taken all of the credit. She absolutely couldn't believe it.

Today her dress was a bright, angular shift that stopped a good four inches above her knees. Her legs were crossed, and the glass-topped table afforded everyone a fantastic view of her boots, which were thigh-high white vinyl. The whole effect was nearly blinding in its brightness. Which may or may not have explained the Carrie Donovan sunglasses perched at the tip of Demetria's nose.

Bishop turned from her post at the head of the table. "Certainly." She and Demetria had worked together for years and, as such, Demetria was the one person with whom Bishop behaved, objectively, "nicely."

"Liv can tell you more about it," Demetria said, flashing a snakelike smile in Liv's direction. Liv's stomach went cold. *Here goes nothing, I suppose,* she decided, swallowing loudly. Could everyone hear her swallowing? It sounded murderously loud in her own head.

From across the table, Gen rolled her eyes. Gen was Bishop's niece, but that hadn't won her any preferential treatment at the magazine—quite the opposite, in fact. Gen was the Beauty intern, but she had wanted the Features beat, which was the most "writerly" and therefore the most posh of the internships. It was also the most competitive slot, and it had gone to Mel. Funnily enough, though, Mel wanted to be what she called a Serious Writer, and didn't really see *Flirt* as much more than a stepping stone. It almost wasn't fair, but then, that was how things tended to work out for Mel. And no one begrudged her her good luck. She was just that likeable. Even her mentor, the notoriously cranky Bishop herself, had taken a shine to the girl.

Olivia couldn't complain. Her parents were old friends of Bishop's, so she was treated quite nicely by the ice queen, as well. Even though it seemed to incur the wrath of Demetria, it did result in being given loads of face time in the office.

"Yes, dear?" Bishop prompted.

Why was Demetria putting her on the spot like this? Olivia merely had an idea; nothing prepared. *Oh dear,* she thought. *Here goes.*

Olivia cleared her throat. "The last three seasons have been about accessible fashion," she said. "Turning the runway into reality. It was a brilliant idea—three seasons ago. But it's time to make fashion more fun again. Very wild, very over-the-top."

"A return to haute couture," Bishop mused aloud. "For the mainstream. Interesting."

"Yes, exactly," Olivia said excitedly, straightening up in her seat.

"Haute and heavy," Demetria cut in. Olivia

> ❝ *It's time to make fashion more fun again.* ❞

looked at Demetria, shocked. That had been her idea, her tagline.

"Beautiful," Bishop said, nodding. "We'll be completely outrageous. It will be all about fun, the exotic, and fantasy."

Olivia just sat there in stunned silence. She looked around at the rest of the staff, who were also nodding their approval. Of course. The idea was brilliant. Her idea.

"We could do some amazing makeup, really bright, unconventional colors," Gen's boss, Naomi, chimed in. Gen nodded instantly. Anything for approval.

"We could focus on, like, extreme sports, or sort of alternatives to the gym," Charlotte suggested. "You know, like those trapeze lessons on the West Side Highway, or Cardio Striptease classes." She giggled. When no one else did, she covered her mouth self-consciously and slid down a bit farther into her seat.

Bishop ignored Charlotte, causing the poor girl to blush furiously. "It's an interesting approach, Demetria," Bishop said.

Liv fought back the urge to say something. But being the proper lady she was, she could say nothing. Nothing at all.

"The idea feels fresh," Demetria said, commanding attention. "I thought I'd work with Lynn on the shoot."

"And perhaps your intern could put together

some copy, maybe a sidebar or two," Bishop added, not using Olivia's name.

There it was. Her assignment.

"If we can pull this together within the next week or so," Bishop continued, "we can run it for September."

"Well, the photography isn't a problem, depending on which models are booked. And Liv can get copy to us stat, right, Liv?" Demetria asked.

"Of course," Liv replied quickly.

"Of course," Kiyoko mimicked in a high-pitched voice. She rolled her eyes dramatically.

Bishop raised an eyebrow in Kiyoko's direction, and Kiyoko shrugged her shoulders innocently. An awkward beat followed. Liv wondered if Bishop was going to say something to the precocious teen, but she just turned back to regard the staff at large again.

"Well, for once, I think we're on to something, and with enough time to do some advance preparation, besides."

❝ *She couldn't believe that Demetria had swooped in and taken all of the credit. She absolutely couldn't believe it.* **❞**

"That won't last," Trey snorted. "It never does."

"Be that as it may. Nicely done, Demetria." Bishop nodded shortly at the editor, eliciting a small wave of fury from Olivia.

"Haute and Heavy" had been *her* idea, and a right good one, at that! She couldn't believe that Demetria had swooped in and taken all of the credit. She absolutely couldn't believe it.

I should say something, she thought again.

But I can't. It would be completely inappropriate for me to show Demetria up in the middle of a staff meeting.

For a moment, the two halves of her conscience wrestled each other. Ultimately, though—and rather predictably, Olivia thought—the angel on her shoulder won out. She simply couldn't do it—she couldn't act out at the office. Dodgy though Demetria's behavior was, Olivia was going to have to grin and bear it.

She bit her lip. Bishop was still going on with the particulars. "Department heads, this theme is for the September issue, so critical dates apply. Please submit concepts for your sections by the end of the day Wednesday." She rose imperiously. "I have a conference call." And then she was gone, leaving a trail of Coco Mademoiselle vapors in her wake.

☙   ☙   ☙   ☙

At lunchtime, all the girls could talk about was Olivia's assignment.

"I can't believe your sidebar is going to run in the September issue!" Mel said, enthusiastic as always. She took a huge bite of her falafel sandwich. The girls were sitting outside, eating their street-vendor lunches on benches and enjoying the bright sunshine. Most employees at *Flirt* ate in the monstrous cafeteria—if you could call poking at a few lettuce leaves eating—but the girls liked to mix it up. Most of them didn't really know from fat-free and didn't care to, either. Other than Gen, that was, and of course, Charlotte.

"Well, it's wonderful news," Olivia agreed, "but we've all gotten assignments directly from Bishop. That's the whole point of the internship, no? We're given a chance to show our talents." Mel had written a piece for Bishop, and Alexa had worked on a photo shoot.

Instantly, Olivia realized her faux pas. But before she could step in and correct her statement, Kiyoko interrupted. "Not *all* of us, lads," she said, waving a wooden chopstick in the air. "And for the record, I can't *believe* you let Demetria get away with taking the credit for 'Haute and Heavy.' We all know you've been thinking about that for weeks now."

"Liv's way too polite to make a stink about something like that," Mel interjected, coming to her friend's defense. "And Keeks, you'll get your assignment soon." Mel was anxiously trying to prevent ruffled feathers, that much was obvious. "It's coming. You totally know that."

Kiyoko shrugged again. She was doing an awful lot of shrugging today, Olivia noticed, most of which was directed toward Olivia

> **66** *Frankly, I'm surprised you went with the whole 'walk on the wild side' bit, lad.* **99**

herself, one way or another. "Frankly, I'm surprised you went with the whole 'walk on the wild side' bit, lad," Kiyoko said. She swept her gaze pointedly over Olivia's outfit: a slim-fitting black pencil skirt, a sleeveless silk blouse, and crocodile-skin mules that came to a dangerous-looking point at the tip. The outfit was gorgeous and perfectly coordinated—right down to Liv's oversize Hermès leather tote—but Kiyoko's point was taken; wild, it was not.

Olivia coughed. "As it happens, Kiyoko, I was hoping you'd be willing to give me some input," she said. She bit her lip. This was a risky road to take—Kiyoko could just as easily be offended as she might be flattered. Mel's brow wrinkled, and Alexa paused mid-bite of hot dog.

After what felt like eons, but was probably more

> **_Her response could hardly be construed as enthusiastic._**

like twelve seconds, Kiyoko spoke. "Sure," she said, noncommittal as ever.

Her response could hardly be construed as enthusiastic, Olivia knew. But it was the best reaction Olivia was going to get. She could take it or leave it. So she decided, for the sake of peace in the loft, to take it.

For now, at least. She'd take it for now.

chapter four

When Liv returned to her desk that afternoon, she was surprised to find an e-mail waiting for her from Phoebe Winters. Phoebe had been texting and phoning her incessantly since the gallery opening. Unfortunately, though Phoebe meant well, she was murderously boring, and talking with her had been a deeply painful, endlessly protracted experience. Good breeding could prepare a person for the demands of a given social situation, but it certainly didn't guarantee any sort of enjoyment of such.

Not to mention, Liv was already in trouble with her mother from that photo that had been taken of her holding *Phoebe's* cocktail. Highly unfair.

From: pwinters@uk-usa.com
To: liv_b-c@flirt.com
Subject: this evening

Hey, Liv—

Do you fancy getting a coffee this evening after work? A group of us are going round to the new place that's opened along Central Park. It's meant to be quite cozy. Anyway, ring me if you're interested.

Ta,
Phoebes

Reading the e-mail, Olivia sighed to herself. She wasn't at all interested in going out with Phoebe and the rest of her friends. But she felt terribly guilty declining an invitation without good reason, and she knew her parents would be disappointed to hear that she had dodged an invite from Phoebe, given their relationship with the Winters family.

She hovered over the keyboard uncertainly.

"Liv, you busy tonight?" It was Mel, breezing by the fashion department bearing approved sketches from Bishop. The darling girl had no idea how perfect her timing could be.

"I don't know yet," Liv said. "Did you have something in mind?"

"It's supposed to, like, pour rain," Mel said, looking depressed at the mere thought of inclement weather. "I say we hole up, watch movies, stuff our faces."

"Brilliant," Olivia replied, grinning. The plan

> **" I say we hole up, watch movies, stuff our faces. "**

sounded fantastic, and would have even if she hadn't been looking for a clean getaway. She quickly wrote back to Phoebe, thanking her graciously for extending the invitation, but explaining that she and her flatmates had plans together for that evening. Done.

"Oh, I almost forgot," Mel said, backtracking from down the hallway. "Bishop wanted me to give you this. Crazy!" Her eyes twinkled as she dropped a newspaper clipping on Liv's desk.

The paper hit the surface of Liv's desk with a soft swishing sound, and suddenly her own face was beaming primly back up at her. It was a "Page Six" shot, taken from the gallery opening; there was Phoebe Winters, leaning daintily into the frame. "It's nothing," Olivia said, a soft blush coloring her cheeks.

"Nothing, are you insane? You're, like, famous!" Mel said, not picking up on Liv's intense desire to downplay the whole sordid ordeal. "Some people would kill to be in 'Page Six.' "

"You're, like, famous!"

Liv shrugged. "I suppose." The truth was, it happened to her all the time. Back home, she could hardly leave the house without her and her family's whereabouts being covered extensively in the local media. And British papers were not known for being tasteful, well-intentioned, or compassionate toward their subjects. Olivia was not only bored by the paparazzi, but she rather detested being captured on film.

"You're a celebrity, Liv," Mel said.

Olivia sighed. "In some circles, I suppose."

She accepted Mel's statement as true, seeing no other option. But that didn't mean she liked it.

☉   ☉   ☉   ☉

"Anchovies?!"

Olivia stepped tentatively into the large, open kitchen of the *Flirt* loft, wondering who was shrieking at the top of her lungs. The day's work was behind her and she was ready to shrug it off, but the screaming was certainly intruding on that plan. It became apparent upon first glance that Mel was the offended party. She stood, hands on hips, nose wrinkled delicately in Kiyoko's direction.

"You said we were making pasta, lad," Kiyoko replied defiantly. "I offered to make the sauce. I distinctly recall saying, 'I'll make the sauce,' to which you replied—"

"I *know* what I 'replied,' " Mel interjected, a bit singsongy on the word. "Because you said that homemade pasta sauce was your specialty. So it seemed like a good idea to let you go to town. Little did I know you'd even think of adding something like"—she shuddered violently—"*anchovies* to the mix. *Blech.*"

"Don't knock it till you've tried it, sister," Kiyoko said, waving the tin of fish dangerously close to Mel. "It's puttanesca sauce, and it completely rocks. I learned how to make it when I was living in Florence." Kiyoko's father was a diplomat; she'd lived in nearly every major city in the world. Except New York, which was why she'd been so keen on winning the *Flirt* internship— "free room and board, baby," as she'd put it. "The sauce completely rocks *if* you add the anchovies."

"Hello, I'm a vegetarian, remember?" Mel asked, her voice as close to edgy as Olivia could recall.

Kiyoko rolled her eyes. "Fish doesn't count."

Mel shook her head vehemently, blond curls bobbing right and left. "No way, no how. I'm not going to do it." She stuck her tongue out. "And if I *were* going to break my vegetarianism? It wouldn't be for *that*." She crossed her arms over her chest as if to say *enough is enough*.

"I have an idea," Olivia chimed in eagerly. Mel was constantly diffusing tension between Olivia and Kiyoko; the least Liv could do was return the favor. "Why don't we order sushi in? There's that place down the street that does lovely sashimi—and they have vegetarian rolls,

And if I were going to break my vegetarianism? It wouldn't be for that.

too, Mel—you remember," she added hastily.

Mel's eyes widened at the thought. "The last time we ordered from there it was, like, twenty dollars for two rolls and a salad," she said.

"Exactly. Dead cheap, right?" Olivia's point exactly. They'd order; they'd eat. Problem solved.

> **Dead cheap, right?**

Kiyoko burst out laughing, and Liv realized her misstep. Twenty dollars was obviously not cheap to Mel. *Well, that's not my fault,* Liv thought indignantly. In England, almost everything cost nearly double what they cost in the States. Her parents' rather cushy budget notwithstanding, she was accustomed to spending quite a bit more on . . . well, just about everything.

"It's just that, in some places, twenty bucks gets you dinner out, not a few tiny pieces of vegetables wrapped in rice," Mel said kindly.

"Right," Olivia said, trying to play it off like she knew exactly what Mel meant. It was easier said than done. She felt right foolish, and she worried that Mel and Kiyoko could sense as much. How embarrassing. "Never mind, then," she conceded. "Let's cook, shall we?" There it was, the frosty edge to her voice that Kiyoko often commented on. She couldn't help it; the frost was how she dealt with uncomfortable situations.

"There's *gotta* be something you can substitute for anchovies," Mel said quickly, obviously trying to move on past the little sushi incident.

"Capers, I *guess,*" Kiyoko said. "Whatever." She disappeared into the pantry to pull out some dry ingredients. "You're just lucky we sent Alexa off in search of the fresh pasta, 'cause she'd take my side in a minute, lad."

"I'll help," Olivia offered, glad to no longer be the focus of attention.

"Great, why don't you get started crushing these tomatoes?" Mel suggested, handing Liv a can and a frightful-looking contraption.

"I'd be glad to do so," Liv said, taking the proffered materials from her friend. "That is, if you'll explain to me just one small thing."

"Of course!" Mel said brightly.

"What is this?" Liv asked, gesturing sadly at the contraption.

Mel laughed so hard, she snorted. "Olivia," she said affectionately. "What are we going to do with you?"

"I don't spend much time in the kitchen back home," Liv admitted. The truth was, her parents had practically a whole battalion of help.

"You don't say," Mel replied drily. "Well, I'm about to rock your world." She took the . . . whatever it

> **66** *This, my dear? This is an electric can opener. And it's going to change your life.* **99**

was . . . out of Liv's hands and placed it on the countertop ceremoniously. "This, my dear? This is an electric can opener. And it's going to change your life."

⟳　　⟳　　⟳　　⟳

From: flyguy@hh.net
To: liv_b-c@flirt.com
Subject: your narrow escape

Hey, Olivia—

　　My wily female friend.
　　While you may have tried to disappear from Friday's party without a trace, my sleuthing skills are top-notch. Yes, it's true, I asked Kiyoko for your e-mail addy. I hope you don't mind.
　　Was wondering if you'd be game to check out a new hip-hop joint downtown Thursday night? I don't know if that's your

scene or whatever, but a buddy of mine is
DJing and I promised I'd stop by.

It'll be good times. This I can assure you.

Lemme know,
Eli

. . . .

From: liv_b-c@flirt.com
To: kiyoko_k@flirt.com
Subject: ?

Kiyoko—

Did you pass my e-mail address on to Eli
on Friday night? After I'd left? Brilliant! Thank
you so much. I had no idea he was keen on
me at all. Guess I'm much less attuned to the
male species than you! He's asked me out for
Thursday, so I think it's a date! I'll be happy to
return the favor, if ever there's a chance.

—Olivia

. . . .

From: kiyoko_k@flirt.com
To: liv_b-c@flirt.com
Subject: Re: ?

Hey, lad—

Who am I to stand in the way of true like? He fancies you, you fancy him . . . go for it.

Enjoy Eli.

No need to return the favor; I've got all the male props I can handle.

—K

. . . .

From: liv_b-c@flirt.com
To: flyguy@hh.net
Subject: Your detecting skills . . .

. . . are spot on! I'm pleased you were able to get my contact information from Kiyoko.

As it happens, I'm free Thursday night and I reckon I'd love to see your friend perform. Do let me know the particulars!

Best,
Olivia

chapter five

"That's it, baby—you've got it! This is all you."

Olivia laughed, watching Jonah Jones hold a ridiculous feathered bodysuit up to a sky-high beanpole of a model. The bodysuit—a bright, canary yellow—was absurd, playful, and extravagant all at once. Sort of like Big Bird re-imagined by Issey Miyake. No normal woman would ever be able to wear something like that in real life. But that was exactly the point of this shoot.

After the staff meeting on Monday, Demetria had immediately made some calls and pulled together some edgy couture pieces for a preliminary photo shoot. They'd try a few poses, sort of a test run, a mini-section to run in the big "Haute and Heavy" issue. Bishop wanted to see a few outtakes before committing to the entire spread. Demetria had asked Olivia to book all of the models for the shoot—and then, surprisingly, asked Olivia to join her for the day.

Possibly, Liv thought, *Demetria feels guilty for taking credit for my idea.* Possibly, but probably not. Liv tried not to dwell on the issue, especially since she'd also come in to work to find another e-mail from Eli waiting for her.

So now it was Wednesday, and Liv had spent the last

three hours helping Jonah pull together bright, colorful pieces in bold and interesting textures while Alexa, Lynn, and the freelance photographers adjusted lighting and snapped Polaroids. Liv couldn't believe that they'd managed to pull this shoot off in less than forty-eight hours.

Now Tatyana Milova, Russia's newest import, was sucking in her cheeks and voguing as Jonah draped the Big Bird suit against her skeletal frame. Tatyana's razor-sharp, peroxided bangs provided just the right contrast for the suit's egg-yolk hue.

"My God, he's mad," Olivia murmured, half to Demetria, half to herself. Only Jonah would have known that Tatyana's sharp angles and stark coloring would be the ideal backdrop for such an eye-catching article of clothing.

"It's true, he's completely gone," Demetria agreed, lighting a cigarette and inhaling deeply. "Thank God for the rest of us."

"Thank God for the rest of us."

Olivia wasn't quite sure what Demetria meant by that—Demetria certainly seemed at least as mad as anyone else—but before she could question it, Demetria was clapping her hands together and speaking through clenched teeth around her cigarette. "Beautiful, folks, great work! Lunch"—she gestured to a lavish catering spread laid out on a long cafeteria-style table—"is served. Take an hour." She mock-glared at the models. "Don't screw up your hair or makeup."

The photographers, makeup artists, hairstylists, and wardrobe consultants smiled and gradually edged toward the table, where they picked at the half sandwiches, removing offending fillings like cheese or deli meat. It made Olivia giggle. In the industry, a girl had to be pretty solid in her sense of self to withstand the pressure to avoid calories at all cost.

Demetria, for her part, was greedily breathing on her cigarette and gulping down huge mouthfuls of vitamin water. "God, I'm tired," she rasped. "You're probably fresh as a daisy," she said, looking Olivia up and down with a resentful glint in her eye. "The full bloom of youth and all."

Olivia nodded uncertainly. "I suppose," she said, demurring.

"Oh, none of this false modesty, sweetie—you're fantastic," Jonah said, sashaying toward the girls while shaking up his own bottle of mineral water. "This stuff has

> ❝ *'You're probably fresh as a daisy,'*
> *she said, looking Olivia up and down*
> *with a resentful glint in her eye.*
> *'The full bloom of youth and all.'* ❞

no caffeine, no energy boost," he said with mild disgust. "What a waste of my time." He took a sip anyway and frowned again. "Can I get one of those, hon?" he asked Demetria, gesturing toward her cigarette.

"I didn't know you smoked," Olivia said with surprise as he puffed away.

"Filthy habit," he said. "But we all smoke on shoots. Want one?"

Olivia shook her head an emphatic no. Fags were one thing she'd managed to avoid entirely, despite their prevalence in Europe. In addition to the fact that her parents would murder her for smoking, there was the fact that, as Jonah said, cigarettes were repulsive.

"Very sweet, very proper, very innocent."

"Very sweet, very proper, very innocent," Jonah said, half-kidding. He collapsed against the prop table, taking care not to disrupt any of the accessories strewn across it. "So," he said, "any thoughts about your sidebar?"

"Yes, do share," Demetria said, leaning forward with interest.

"To be honest, I'm still just tossing some ideas around," Liv said, feeling tentative. She hadn't come up with any surefire concepts, though she did have the germ of a thought or two. But Jonah and Demetria seemed so interested, and one couldn't discount the importance of having their undivided attention. It was worth bouncing some ideas off of them. "What about . . . 'animal instincts'?" she ventured. "You know, like the different prints, textures, and fabrics that we use in couture that are inspired by wildlife."

Silence. Somewhere in the distance, crickets chirped.

Slightly daunted, Olivia cleared her throat and forged onward. "For instance, leopard or tiger print, fur—real *or* faux"—she amended hastily—"crocodile skin . . ." she trailed off, utterly cowed by their lack of enthusiasm. "What do you think?" she finished lamely.

The looks on their faces was answer enough. Still, to Jonah's credit, he rallied. "That's an interesting . . . start," he ventured. "But I wonder if you wouldn't be better off pursuing something more . . . innovative?"

"Exactly," Demetria agreed, nodding like a dashboard bobblehead. She was clearly thrilled to have someone else's phrasing to latch on to. "It's just that . . .

> **The looks on their faces was answer enough. I wonder if you wouldn't be better off pursuing something more . . . innovative?**

animal prints have been done, you know, to death."

She doesn't have to seem so smug *about it,* Olivia thought. It was as though Demetria wanted Olivia to fail.

Olivia bit her lip. She *did* know that animal prints were old news, certainly. But she didn't have any better ideas at present. What was she going to do?

Kiyoko was right, Liv thought glumly. *I'm all wrong for this assignment.*

It didn't matter that Liv had enough pocket money to keep herself in designer duds. Her personal sense of style was quiet, understated, and classic. And breaking out of that shell was going to be harder than she ever imagined. Honestly, she wasn't completely sure she could do it.

Ms. Bishop will be so disappointed, Liv thought. Which meant that her parents would be, as well.

☙   ☙   ☙   ☙

After the shoot wrapped, Olivia and Alexa stayed behind tidying up. One of their jobs as interns was to take the props back to the office, where they'd be relegated to The Closet, where all sorts of fabulous, stylish accessories and clothing lived. Magazine editors—and particularly fashion magazine editors—were expected to walk the walk, which meant being very up-to-the-minute at all

> **Back in her streetwear, Tatyana looked much more like a regular person, albeit a freakishly tall, impossibly thin, and arrestingly good-looking regular person.**

times. Designers and vendors were constantly showering Bishop and her staff with samples, which they collected, organized, and stored away for a rainy day.

Alexa fawned over a pair of stiletto Jimmy Choo mules. "Did we even use these in the shoot?" she asked. "*Mira*, I can't remember. It was all a blinding flash of lights, cameras, and—"

"—feathers." It was Tatyana Milova, emerging from the dressing area. Back in her streetwear, Tatyana looked much more like a regular person, albeit a freakishly tall, impossibly thin, and arrestingly good-looking regular person. "Don't forget the feathers." Her accent added an interesting dimension to the content of her words. "You did good today, both of you," she said sweetly. "This is your first . . ."—she struggled to come up with the word—"internship?"

"*Sí,*" Alexa said, excited to be talking to a real, live supermodel as though she were just a plain old human being.

"*Flirt* is a great first job," Tatyana said knowingly.

"I was fourteen when I came to New York from Russia, and *Flirt* was the first cover I ever did. It was amazing exposure."

"Right after that, your career took off," Liv said, remembering.

"Yes. And now here I am again. No matter how busy I get, I always make time for Josephine Bishop. You should remember that," she said. "Bishop gets things done. She's a VIP, you know?"

"Yes, we know," Liv said, laughing. Even supermodels worshipped Bishop—or rather, super-models *especially* worshipped Bishop. "Quite right?"

"Oh, you are English?" Tatyana asked. "I love the accent."

"I like yours, too," Liv said shyly.

"And"—Tatyana leaned in and reached out to brush Olivia's earlobe—"I *love* these earrings."

Olivia reached up to touch her ears, trying to remember which earrings she'd put on that morning. They were small, delicate beaded chandeliers. "Thanks," she said. "I made them myself."

"You made them?" Tatyana asked, looking pleasantly surprised.

Liv nodded. "Yes, beadwork is a hobby of mine. Everything you see in the stores is either too boring, or too over-the-top."

"Well, these, my friend, are just right," Tatyana said

with finality. She glanced at her watch. "I have to meet my boyfriend," she explained, almost apologetically. "He gets cranky when I keep him waiting."

"Men," Alexa groaned sympathetically.

Tatyana chuckled and rolled her eyes. "Right? Well, good work today! And congratulations on getting an internship at *Flirt*!"

Msg received at 3:43 PM from: PrincessGen

How's the shoot? Just got invited to a fab beauty party 2night at Underbar. Char's busy: Auntie B said 2 take U! Wanna come?

Msg sent at 4:15 PM from: LondonCalling

Brill! Tell B thx for the invite! Meet you back at loft.

chapter six

"Y ou're doing *what* tonight?" Alexa shrieked.

"Shh, she'll hear you. It's not polite," Olivia chided, imploring Alexa to keep her voice down.

"Mira, lo siento," Alexa said hurriedly, lowering her voice an octave or two. "It's just that I *thought* you said you were going to a party with Miss Pretty Princess tonight! Crazy! *Loca en la cabeza*!" she cried, her voice rising as she got agitated all over again.

"She's not *that* bad," Olivia protested. "Besides, evidently Ms. Bishop specifically asked her to invite me to this party. I can hardly say no to that, don't you think?" Liv realized as she spoke that now she had Bishop dictating her social life in addition to her parents' demands. This was all going completely pear-shaped. Was there any part of her life that was actually her own these days? She sighed and leaned backward on her bed, hugging a throw pillow to her chest.

"If Bishop suggested it, you can't say no," Alexa agreed grudgingly. "But I bet it was all Gen's idea. Her lifelong dream is to

Was there any part of her life that was actually her own these days?

get in 'Page Six,' and she knows that won't happen unless she's accompanied by one Miss Olivia Bourne-Cecil." Alexa was camped out, Indian-style, on Charlotte's bed. As Gen had said in her text message earlier, Charlotte was busy. She was out researching a story on all-soy diets. It sounded right awful, and included some sort of overnight stay at a spa downtown. A spa that only served soy-based food. *Blech.*

"But I don't trust Gen for a minute," Alexa went on. Gen and Alexa were locked in a sort of ongoing grudge match, and had been ever since Alexa had featured Gen on her blog in a not-so-flattering light. Liv felt that the postings were well-deserved, but the ensuing rivalry was somewhat counterproductive. Still, she completely understood Alexa's point, and recognized that Gen's motives were generally not very purely driven.

"Your point is well-taken, Alexa," Liv assured her. "Don't worry. I won't forget about any of the things that she's done to us girls. But I'm going to this party. So I'll need you to help me sort out an outfit." She smiled slyly. "This evening, I'll need to walk on the wild side."

"Awesome!" Alexa clapped her hands together. "I can lend you my leopard-print camisole."

Olivia frowned. "Right, then. Not *that* wild. Forget that. How about walking on the 'more outgoing than usual' side?"

Alexa sighed. "We'll find you something."

" *Not that wild. Forget that. How about walking on the 'more outgoing than usual' side?* **"**

❧   ❧   ❧   ❧

"I *love* your shoes," Gen gushed.

"Thank you," Olivia said primly, feeling slightly self-conscious but appreciating the compliment. In the end, she'd worn a pair of perfectly cut jeans and a black silk halter top with an asymmetrical, handkerchief cut. Alexa had loaned her a pair of pink wedges in mock crocodile skin that added a tiny hint of flair to an otherwise safe, utterly "Olivia" ensemble. Although the shoes were mainly covered by the wide legs of her jeans, Liv still felt as though she were wearing neon on her feet. She just had to face it: Adventurous was really not her thing.

But it needs to be, Liv thought, *if I'm meant to impress Bishop and the likes of them with my sidebar. No more pencil skirts and kitten-heeled mules.*

Liv looked around the party for inspiration. It wasn't happening here. This was a launch party for a new face cream, not a fashion show, and that was reflected by the turnout.

The party was held at Underbar, a bar located, fittingly enough, on the sublevel of the W hotel in Union Square. It wasn't the trendiest location, but the bar was all mood lighting and smooth, polished surfaces, and most models in New York City lived and breathed downtown. Clearly, almost all of them had been invited to this party. But they were far outnumbered by clusters of identically clad beauty editors in pointed-toe shoes and super-dark, premium denim.

Looking around, Liv saw uniformed waiters and waitresses passing signature martinis around on trays, as well as miniscule, arty-pretty little canapés. No one was eating the canapés. Liv had helped herself to exactly one shrimp puff when she first arrived and scarfed it down discreetly, facing a wall. Gen, of course, didn't do carbs.

The well-groomed editors laughed high-pitched, tinkling laughs as they gestured grandly with perfectly manicured fingertips. The scene was a blinding collage of skimpy black tops, shimmering makeup, and flowing, glowing highlights. Gen, Olivia noted, was well in her

" The scene was a blinding collage of skimpy black tops, shimmering makeup, and flowing, glowing highlights. "

element, tossing her glossy brunette mane with the best of them and smiling widely to expose her perfect toothpaste-ad white teeth. She was chatting up an editor-in-chief of a well-known magazine whom Olivia recognized. Liv knew that Gen would do anything to be a model. But while the girl was certainly beautiful, she was far too short to ever do runway work. Maybe beauty shoots were the way to go—after all, a great head of hair was a great head of hair, no matter how long one's legs were.

Liv sidled up to Gen's conversation, careful not to actually interrupt. That would be dreadfully rude. Gen smiled brightly when she noticed that she had company.

"Hey there!" Gen chirped. "I was just talking about you. This is Mona Sloan, the editor-in-chief of *Gloss* magazine . . ." She waved her arm in the direction of Mona. Liv couldn't help but notice that Gen didn't seem to have the greatest control over her arm. In fact, her limbs were swaying like overcooked pasta.

"And Mona," Gen said, swallowing loudly, "this is Olivia Bourne-Cefil. I mean, *Cefil*." She hiccupped. "Cecil. But we call her Lizzie."

"It's actually Liv," Olivia said awkwardly, extending her hand to shake. Mona held her own out in response, casting a questioning sidelong glance in Gen's direction. "Lovely to meet you."

"Are you also an intern at *Flirt*?" Mona asked.

"Yesshh, indeed. She is the fashion intern," Gen cut in. "And my Auntie Jo just *loves* her." She stumbled briefly. "Whoops," she said, regaining her footing and grinning. "Heels." She shrugged.

"Gen, are you feeling all right?" Olivia asked worriedly, wondering what had gotten into her sort-of friend.

"Oh, sure," Gen said breezily. "But—I need another drink. Have you had one of those martinis? They're sour apple. Like the face cream. Tastes great. The martinis, I mean. Not the face cream." She giggled, then hiccupped again. Loudly.

Oh, dear, Liv thought. Obviously Gen had enjoyed one too many sour apple martinis. It was the specialty drink of the party, in celebration of the face cream in question, which was made with "the soothing powers of green-apple extract." Or so read the press release, anyway.

That was the problem with most Americans, Olivia knew—since the legal drinking age in the U.S. was so much older than it was in Europe, most teens sneaked about and therefore had no idea how to hold their drink. It was a good thing that Olivia didn't care to do much more than sip socially on rare occasions. One of them needed to be coherent at a professional event like this, and clearly, that wasn't going to be Gen.

Quickly, Liv turned to Mona. "If you'll excuse us for a moment, I'm just going to find myself a glass of water." She didn't want to make a thing about Gen's inebriated state, but if they stuck around much longer, it would be fairly unavoidable. As it was, Mona was nodding conspiratorially toward Liv as Gen's head slumped downward toward her chest.

"I think that's a great plan," Mona said dryly. "You're a good friend."

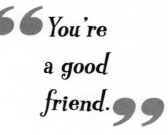
"You're a good friend."

"I suppose I am," Liv said, under her breath. It didn't matter that Mona couldn't hear her. She was talking to herself more than anything else.

ⓖ　　ⓖ　　ⓖ　　ⓖ

"Where we goin'?" Gen slurred, half-walking, half-allowing Olivia to drag her across the main area of the lounge. She was starting to resemble a tabloid shot of a party-hearty starlet: heavy-lidded eyes, smeared makeup, mussed hair.

"We're just going to pop into the loo for a moment," Olivia said, taking care not to let her exasperation or her concern show on her face. The last thing either of the girls needed was to make a scene. "I think you need a

> **"I don't believe the room is moving."**

splash of cold water."

"Thassa good idea," Gen said. "The room is moving, did you know?"

"I don't believe it is, but I can see why you might feel that way," Olivia replied. "Gen, how many of those martinis did you drink, anyway? You're well pissed."

"Just the one."

"One?" Olivia found that hard to believe. As it was, Gen was rapidly losing control of her motor skills.

"One, and then another one, and then another one."

Okay, three, and they'd been at the party for about two hours. That was exactly enough alcohol to wreak havoc on Gen's zero percent body-fat frame. And then some.

"Here we go," Olivia said, maneuvering the bathroom door open with her hip and scooting Gen in. She dragged the girl over to the sink and turned the cold water on. "Look, they've got little paper cups," Liv said. She filled one with some lukewarm water. "Drink."

Gen gulped the water down in one swallow and then collapsed onto a chaise lounge propped against the far end of the bathroom. "So tired."

Just then the door to one of the individual stalls opened, and out walked Tatyana Milova. "You again!" she said, clearly recognizing Olivia from the afternoon shoot and pleased to see her. "Having fun?" Tatyana looked as though she was quite enjoying the party herself; her cheeks were flushed and her eyes sparkled.

"I'm afraid some of us are having too much fun," Olivia said, fretful. "We've got to go home soon."

"I understand," Tatyana said, glancing dubiously over at Gen's semiconscious figure. "I've been there myself. Sometimes you're the caretaker, sometimes you're the one being taken care of, no?"

Olivia laughed. "Quite right," she said. "But I'm glad we came."

"The gift bags are phenomenal, right?" Tatyana asked. "Did you see they have that new lip balm made with pulverized crystals? I have been dying to try that— but I would never pay one hundred dollars for a fancy lip balm, you know?"

"Really?" Olivia asked, slightly incredulous. One hundred dollars seemed perfectly reasonable for something that contained actual crystals. And she didn't think supermodels were ones to haggle over money.

"Please," Tatyana said, rolling her eyes. "Some of the best-kept beauty secrets are, how do you say . . . dirt cheap." She fished into her tiny clutch and pulled

"Some of the best-kept beauty secrets are, how do you say . . . dirt cheap."

out a tube of mascara in lurid pink-and-green plastic. "This? Less than ten bucks. Best ever." She fluttered her eyelashes in Olivia's direction. "Every model knows about this. Deals are out there. You just have to look for them." She shrugged. "I take my makeup off at night with Vaseline, you know?"

Olivia nodded, pretending to have an idea of what Tatyana was talking about. Every year, Liv's mother took her to Marks and Spencer to have her colors done. She'd never owned a ten-dollar mascara in her life. She knew they existed, of course, but she'd never really *seen* a tube up close like this. It was a little bit like seeing a UFO. And she wasn't completely sure what Vaseline was. Maybe they called it something else in the U.K.

"I don't feel so great," Gen said suddenly, interrupting Olivia's lesson in bargain beauty.

"Oh!" Olivia cried, suddenly remembering the initial problem. She turned to Tatyana apologetically. "I should really get her home."

"Of course," the model said, tossing her hair over her shoulder. "Water should do it, and maybe some aspirin before she goes to sleep."

"*Perfecto,*" Gen whispered. "You're very tall, didja know that?" She tilted her head crazily toward Olivia. "Models are very tall. Makes me feel short."

So that was it, Liv realized. Gen had been feeling insecure. She'd probably downed her first drink too

> **She'd never owned a ten-dollar mascara in her life. She knew they existed, of course, but she'd never really seen a tube up close like this. It was a little bit like seeing a UFO.**

quickly while talking to some VIP, and it had all gone downhill from there. Well, this was a story without a happy ending—save for some gorgeous gift bags and some beauty tips from the professionals.

"You're not short," Olivia said kindly, hoisting Gen up by the waist and leading her gently out of the bathroom. "At least, not too short."

As though Gen would even remember this conversation once the night was over.

❦   ❦   ❦   ❦

Outside the bathroom the party was in full swing. This was a good thing, as it allowed the girls to slip out unnoticed. Or, almost unnoticed.

"What happened to her?" some fresh young twentysomething screamed, leaning his smooth, unlined face close to Olivia's.

Liv shrank back. "We're fine, thank you," she answered politely. "We'll just be getting a cab." Somewhere in the distance, a flashbulb went off. Gen squinted and groaned, and Olivia quickly moved forward again.

🌀　　🌀　　🌀　　🌀

It only took a few minutes to get a cab, and before she knew it, Olivia was settled into the backseat with Gen, heading downtown toward the loft. Gen was moaning quietly, and Liv only hoped the girl would be able to hold off being sick; it'd be utterly humiliating to lose it in the back of a taxi. Liv sighed and brushed her hair back from her face, then sat up straight. "Gen, it's twelve thirty!" Their curfew on weeknights was eleven, unless they called in special permission. Which they had not done this evening. "Emma's going to murder us!"

"Ssss'all right. We can sneak in the fire escape," Gen mumbled, mentioning their preferred method of flying under the radar.

"You can't be serious," Olivia replied. "You're in no position to climb, and I certainly can't carry you."

They turned a corner, and the loft came into view. Gen was giggling softly to herself. "Silly Olivia," she said. "Don't be ridiculous. Emma goes to bed early. She'll never, never know."

"I reckon you're wrong about that," Liv said, a sinking feeling settling into her stomach. "And you're about to see why."

The cab came to a smooth stop just in front of the loft, and Liv's insides did another panicky backflip. The light in Emma's window, which faced the street, was on. But worse than that? The shadow of Emma herself, peeking out.

chapter seven

From: liv_b-c@flirt.com
To: flyguy@hh.net
Subject: Big apologies

Hello!

I'm so sorry to be writing you at the last minute, but I'm afraid I'm going to have to postpone our plans for the evening. Don't ask; it makes for a better story in person, but suffice it to say I'm currently under house arrest.

I am free, however, at the weekend, barring further "incident."

—Olivia

. . . .

From: flyguy@hh.net
To: liv_b-c@flirt.com
Subject: no apology necessary . . .

. . . as long as you swear you'll fill me in on the

details of what promises to be a very intriguing story.

Let's say tomorrow night. Eight-ish. We can still see some hip-hop, though my friend won't be spinning. Which I guess just means I'll have to be that much more captivating in order to hold your attention.

—E

. . . .

From: liv_b-c@flirt.com
To: flyguy@hh.net
Subject: brilliant

See you tomorrow! Feel free to ring me with the details.

. . . .

"I cannot *believe* we are, like, *grounded*! And on a Thursday night! Ugh. Doesn't Emma, like, know that Thursday is technically the start of the weekend? I mean, how can you ground someone over the weekend?" Gen shook her head at the injustice of it all.

It was indeed Thursday night, and Gen and Olivia were grounded as punishment for missing curfew

"You do the crime, you do the time."

the night before. While Olivia wasn't thrilled about the situation, she did understand that they had broken the rules and therefore warranted punishment. As Mel had said, "You do the crime, you do the time." Of course, dear Mel had been thoughtful enough to espouse this theory before heading off to a movie screening for the evening. Olivia didn't mind too much, however, particularly given that she'd been able to reschedule her date with Eli, so there was no real damage done to her social life.

Truth be told, she rather enjoyed the idea of a quiet night in. She'd never met anyone quite like Eli before—he was larger than life, really—and she quite fancied some extra time to get her thoughts together before they went out. She was nervous, actually, to be alone with him. Plus, a night in meant time to work on her sidebar. If she could come up with an idea, that was.

Gen, however, was taking her grounding as a personal insult, and chose to spend the evening swanning around the loft in a pair of velour track pants and a double-layer tank top, moaning loudly about her lot in life.

"This is *so* unfair," she whimpered, stalking from the living room to her bedroom to the kitchen and back again, slamming doors loudly and being sure to stomp her feet as forcefully as possible. Gen had somehow managed to coerce Charlotte, back from the soy spa, to stay in with her, and the two girls were concocting elaborate face masks out of various forms of pureed produce. The only other person in the house was, quite oddly, Kiyoko, who had claimed to need to "recharge her batteries" after an especially crazed few nights out. She had been holed up in her bedroom for nearly the entire evening.

"This is *so wrong*," Gen reiterated for good measure. She flopped down on the huge sectional sofa, taking care, at least, not to leave a trail of green gunk on the upholstery. Her brown eyes peeped through the layer of . . . well, whatever it was, making her look like a cartoon character of sorts.

"What *is* that on your face?" Olivia asked, taking care not to outright laugh at the girl. Gen could be so sensitive, after all.

"It's a green-tea-and-avocado mask. Great for the pores," Gen retorted huffily, folding her arms across her chest. "You could try one," she added pointedly.

"I'm fine, thanks," Olivia replied. *Gen is lucky Alexa isn't home,* she thought. Otherwise, there'd be no stopping the girl from posting a picture of this bare-bones beauty ritual on her blog. As much as Alexa had sworn to turn over a new leaf, Olivia knew that the sight of Gen with a pound of guacamole slathered across her face would be utterly too tempting to resist.

Olivia walked past the two goo-faced girls and headed into her room to work. But after exactly ten minutes of staring at the wall, she gave up. Her mind was a complete and utter blank. Olivia walked over to her dresser and picked up a bracelet she'd been working on, a wrist cuff made from knots of woven silk. It was a variation on the leather cuffs she'd seen at the stalls of every SoHo street vendor—more colorful and, of course, more personal. "What do you think?" she asked Gen, walking into the living room. "Would you wear this?"

"I suppose," Gen sniffed. Olivia knew that coming from the ice princess, this was high praise. Gen was incredibly insecure and woefully jealous, and therefore not one to easily dispense compliments. Clearly, she loved the bracelet.

"I could show you how to make one," Liv offered. She was as suspicious of Gen as her roommates were, but there wasn't any reason to be overly frosty to the girl. After all, they were both stuck at home, weren't they? Okay, Liv had to admit it—she *was* procrastinating, but anyway, she was making a point of trying to be friendlier these days. She'd started with Eli—and look how well that had gone.

Gen shrugged. "Dunno. Charlotte's going to do a moisturizing treatment for my hair, too, so . . ."

As if on cue, Charlotte sauntered out of the kitchen. At this point, Olivia could barely suppress her amusement at the sight of the girl. She was practically a Gen clone right now, subbing black velour trousers for Gen's lilac set, and a gray cashmere sweater instead of the tank tops. Liv wondered briefly if the girls had coordinated their outfits beforehand. Of course, what made them look most alike was the face masks, which looked increasingly hilarious as they hardened.

"Maybe we should do this in the bathroom, Gen," Charlotte began, stirring a wooden spoon vigorously in a plastic bowl. Olivia couldn't see what was in the bowl from where she was sitting, but it didn't smell like roses.

"Don't be silly," Gen said. "I mean, I can put a towel down if you think it's *necessary*, but . . ." her tone of voice indicated exactly how ridiculous she thought that plan was.

"Never mind," Charlotte said timidly, looking quite ashamed of her rather reasonable suggestion.

"You know what? I reckon a towel's a brilliant idea," Olivia said, popping up from the couch and heading off to the closet where the girls stored their linens.

"But Gen said—" Charlotte protested. She stepped forward toward Olivia.

"Never mind that," Olivia said as politely as she could muster. She might have been okay with a

66 *Oooh, You should clean that up right away.* 99

night's grounding, but she didn't fancy having her sentence extended due to a nasty spill of some barely recognizable substance. She tried to maneuver herself around Charlotte, who was blocking the doorway like a half-crazed crusader. Liv sidestepped—

—and crashed directly into Charlotte's bowl of goop. Which was now overturned, and sliding precariously down the leg of Olivia's cashmere bottoms. "Oh, dear," she muttered, before she could stop herself. "That'll leave a stain for sure."

"Oooh," Gen cooed from her perch on the couch, sounding not one bit sorry. "You should clean that up right away." She didn't move a muscle or otherwise indicate that she planned to help.

Liv sighed. "Yes, I will. Straightaway."

ⓖ　　ⓖ　　ⓖ　　ⓖ

The problem was, Olivia wasn't one for doing things like, well . . . laundry. Back home, her parents had a cleaner who took care of that sort of thing, and since Liv had been in New York, she'd had her clothes sent out to be washed. She supposed she could take the trousers to the dry cleaner in the morning, but what if the stain set between now and then?

What was one supposed to do for a stain? Dab it in cold water? Dab it in hot water? Dab it in seltzer water? Leave it alone? She had absolutely no idea. Humiliating, that.

It was too bad that Mel wasn't home. Mel was the type of girl who probably knew how to wash clothes. Or if she didn't, she'd figure it out. She was resourceful that way. *God, I'm sodding useless,* Liv thought. What good was a knowledge of, for instance, which fork was the salad fork when she couldn't even get a stain out of her own trousers? She glanced back toward where Charlotte and Gen were sitting on the couch, laughing and lathering each other's hair in the remains of whatever it was that was soaking into Olivia's pants. Those two would be absolutely no help whatsoever, that much was clear. Which left . . .

God, I'm sodding useless.

Well, Alexa and Mel were out for the evening; Mel at the movie screening and Alexa off hanging out with Ben. Emma was tucked away in her apartment, which was adjacent to but separate from the loft. Liv had no idea where Emma's son, Nick, was, but odds were he was off with his reed-thin, model-gorgeous girlfriend.

So then . . .

> **"Liv had no idea where Emma's son, Nick, was, but odds were he was off with his reed-thin, model-gorgeous girlfriend."**

It was Kiyoko. Kiyoko or bust. And as much as Olivia knew that these trousers weren't obscenely overpriced, they were in fact her favorites for lounging and therefore she was inclined to save, rather than merely replace, them. It was only a stain, after all.

She tentatively knocked on the door to the bedroom that Kiyoko shared with Alexa. No answer. She rapped again, a bit more firmly this time. "Oi, lad, come in!" Kiyoko shouted. "What's the what?"

Olivia pushed the door open and stepped in. She was greeted by the sight of Kiyoko sitting at her small desk, hunched over her gorgeous titanium iBook, oversize headphones resting on her shoulders, and music-splicing program open on the screen. Kiyoko was a genius with music and electronics, so it made sense that on the rare night in, she hung around working on or with both. Although frankly, Olivia couldn't believe Kiyoko wasn't outside painting the town something wild. Liv could see how Eli and Kiyoko would be friends—even from the little that she knew of both of them.

"Er, I'm sorry to bother you," Liv began, hesitant,

as always, around the force of nature that was Kiyoko. She held out her right leg. "But I've had a bit of an incident."

"And?" Kiyoko asked. "Do you want me to lick it clean or something?"

Olivia stiffened. "Of course not," she said, forcing a smile to her lips. "It's just that . . . well, I'm afraid that the trousers will be ruined if they aren't cleaned straightaway, and . . . well, to be perfectly honest, I've no idea how to run the washing machine."

Kiyoko nodded, gazing solemnly at Olivia for a beat or two. Then she burst out laughing. After a moment, she pulled herself together, dabbing at the corners of her eyes. "Okay, lad, it's cool. I'm sorry, I suppose lots of people could find themselves in this situation. I suppose." She said it like she didn't much believe it to be true, but what could Olivia do at this point? "Here's the thing—those are cashmere, right?"

Olivia nodded.

"Yeah, you can't machine-wash cashmere."

"Well, what, then? Should I wait until the dry cleaner opens tomorrow?"

Kiyoko shook her head emphatically. "Whatever this was—"

"—face mask," Olivia offered.

"It's not, like, red wine or chocolate or anything. It'll come out. You just have to hand-wash it." At the

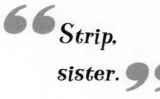**"Strip, sister."** look on Olivia's face, she scooted underneath her bed and rummaged around for a moment or two. She emerged triumphantly, waving a bottle of Woolite. "Strip, sister," Kiyoko commanded.

"Pardon?" Olivia asked, eyes wide.

Kiyoko sighed. "You must have something else to wear while we wash this out, yeah? Or were you thinking you'd hop into the bathtub while I scrub away?"

"Oh!" Liv replied, coloring. "Of course."

She dashed off into her own bedroom to find something suitable to wear.

Half an hour later, Liv's cashmere trousers were rinsed, wrung, and gently hung on a hanger over the bathtub to dry. She only hoped that no one would need to use the bath before they were dry, but seeing as hardly anyone was home, she was probably safe. The leg of her trousers was dark where she scrubbed at it with Woolite, but one could tell that the offending stain was gone. "Thanks so much, Kiyoko, really," she gushed shyly. "I'm right embarrassed at having needed a tutorial in washing clothes."

"You should be," Kiyoko jibed, winking. "No worries, friend. We all have our moments." She paused for a minute, thoughtful. "Well, not me, of course. But whatever." She shrugged good-naturedly. "What were you doing, anyhow? Drinking raw eggs and milk?"

Olivia frowned. "No, though I think Gen and Charlotte may have been."

Kiyoko nodded knowingly. "And you got caught in the crossfire?"

"Exactly. I was working on a bracelet. Thankfully, that escaped intact—unlike my trousers."

"Really? I thought those earrings you were sporting the other day were a one-off, lad," Kiyoko said.

Olivia was surprised. She hadn't expected that Kiyoko would notice her jewelry or know that it was handmade. Then again, the girl had a keen eye for fashion. "No, it's always been a hobby of mine. I think personalized jewelry can rather dress up a proper, traditional wardrobe, don't you think?" She smiled to show Kiyoko that indeed, she was good-naturedly taking the piss out of herself here. "My own wardrobe can certainly stand it."

"You said it, not me," Kiyoko said, grinning teasingly.

"You know—" Olivia began. "I have something that might be perfect for you. Would you care to have a look at it?"

"Pressies for me?" Kiyoko asked. "What girl would say no?"

❝*It's a sort of throwback to New Wave.***❞**

Liv laughed and led Kiyoko across the hallway. Once there, she shimmied under her own bed and pulled out a storage box. She flipped it open and fished out a pair of oversize hoop earrings. Bright, multicolored beads dangled from the earrings, and a tiny white feather sat in the middle of each hoop. "It's a sort of throwback to New Wave," Olivia said, all at once feeling rather uncertain. "I was inspired after that shoot with the model and the feathered dress. But I'd never have an occasion to wear anything like this."

"Really?" Kiyoko asked, snatching the earrings out of Olivia's hand and holding them up to the light. "They're incredible! Totally eighties! I'm going to wear them with my turquoise leg warmers in an homage to Cyndi Lauper."

"Do you like them, then?"

"Are you kidding?" Kiyoko asked. "They're great, really. You're really talented." She shook her head. "I guess I can sort of see why you got the Fashion internship. There's more to you than silk shifts and button-downs."

"Thank you," Olivia said, surprised by this outpouring of warmth.

Was it possible that the two polar opposites were finally starting to come together?

An insistent beeping sound broke the moment. Olivia glanced at her bed to see that her mobile phone was flashing. She had a voice message, she knew. It'd been there for a few hours. She wasn't in any rush to check it. "My parents," she grumbled.

"They know about the grounding?" Kiyoko asked.

"Well, yes, but not directly," Olivia explained. "Rather, they saw my photo in some gossip rag. Me carrying Gen out over my shoulder from that party last night. Lord only knows how they even got the news so quickly. Ms. Bishop must have faxed it over to them personally."

"But *you* were carrying Gen. As in, you weren't the one who was totally soused. So what's their deal?"

"It wasn't 'proper' or 'becoming,'" Olivia mimicked, somewhat surprised by the sharp tone her voice had taken on. "It doesn't reflect well on a family of our standing."

"I get that," Kiyoko said. "My parents are okay, but we're still in the public eye a lot. So I have to keep it together when there are cameras around." She grinned. "And you know it's not always so easy for me to keep it together."

"I hadn't noticed," Olivia said.

"Ignore the message. It's too late to call England now, anyway," Kiyoko said. "Tell me, what did Eli say

"It certainly didn't make Liv feel any less lonely."

when you canceled your date with him?"

"Oh, well, not so much, really," Olivia explained. "We just postponed it for a night." Right away, Liv could tell she'd said the wrong thing. Kiyoko, who just moments before had been giggling and giving her all sorts of girly advice, bristled slightly. Was she jealous of sharing her friend with Olivia? It was ridiculous, but it was the only plausible explanation.

Well. Olivia wanted to be friendlier with Kiyoko, naturally, but she wasn't willing to sacrifice a date with Eli to do so. That was just an unfair expectation on the part of Liv's would-be mate.

Olivia knew she was right, that Kiyoko was being bratty and unreasonable, but it didn't make her feel any better when Kiyoko raised an eyebrow and said, "Oh, well. Enjoy, then. I've, uh, got to get back to my music," and flounced out of the room.

And it certainly didn't make Liv feel any less lonely.

chapter eight

By Friday night, the last thing on Olivia's mind was Kiyoko, and whatever issues the girl may or may not have with Liv's date with Eli. She'd had butterflies in her stomach all morning long—to the detriment of her work at *Flirt*, unfortunately— and had recruited Mel and Alexa to raid The Closet for a suitably understated but fetching outfit. She had to look fantastic but effortlessly so, as though she wasn't at all trying too hard.

Now she sat across from Eli at a Latin restaurant in Alphabet City, off in the nether regions of Avenue C. She had to admit, she'd had her doubts about this neighborhood, but the restaurant itself was charming: an open and airy place with European-style tiled floors, lazy ceiling fans, and wide French doors propped open to allow in the fresh summer air.

Well, semifresh air, at any rate. This *was* Manhattan, after all.

"How did you find this place?" Olivia asked, smiling goofily at her dinner date. Eli was nothing like the boys back home, all of whom were tiny Prince Williams and Harrys in the making: pasty skin and blunt-cut hair, with loud, obnoxious guffawing. Her parents' idea of a suitable partner for her was deeply unappealing.

Eli, though—he was another matter entirely. Tonight he wore a pair of brown corduroys and a subdued plaid button-down shirt. Over that he'd thrown a comfortable-looking cream sweater vest, and on his feet he wore yet another limited-edition pair of Puma trainers. He was even sporting a pair of horn-rimmed glasses, which he hadn't had on at the party. The glasses lent his playful look an element of curiosity. Olivia was well charmed; not only did Eli have a distinctly "American" look, but he had the personality to back it up, too. Or at least, he'd had it so far.

"My roommate is Cuban, and he's always looking for a place that knows how to make chorizo," Eli explained. "Whenever a new Latin place opens up, we have to check it out. He gave this one his stamp of approval."

"Well, in that case, I suppose we're meant to order the chorizo," Liv replied. "Which sounds perfect. I also think the shrimp sautéed in garlic would be quite nice."

"You're kidding," Eli said. He burst out laughing. "A girl who looks like you eats sausage and shrimp covered with oil?" He shook his head in disbelief. "I think you're my dream date."

Olivia flushed. She

> **I think you're my dream date.**

certainly hoped so. "It's not very ladylike now, is it, to have a big appetite," she mused. "But there's no one here to check up on me right now—and I'm assuming you won't say anything?" She arched an eyebrow in his direction, and he nodded his agreement. "You should see the models who come to the shoots," she continued. "Toothpick-thin. Rather alarming. Today, one came in for a go-see, I think she was eight feet tall. But apparently, she'd gained some weight since they first called her to come in. It was a travesty. Though I, for one, thought she looked fantastic." Liv rolled her eyes, recalling Bishop's appalled reaction to the model's size-two frame.

"Good thing you're keeping your head about it all," he said. "It's different in school, of course, but I get where you're coming from. At NYU, I gotta tell you, it's mad competitive. People don't even want to share their notes with you if you miss a day of school. I don't ever want to be like that, but sometimes it's hard to maintain my perspective."

"I didn't realize your course was so rigorous," Olivia said. "That's dead impressive."

"Dead impressive," he mimicked her accent good-naturedly. "Well, I only do it to get the girls. Anyway, that's why I'm around this summer—taking extra courses. You have no idea how many requirements there are."

"I can imagine." She cleared her throat. "So, how do you know Kiyoko?"

"Keeks? I met her sister while I was traveling in Europe last summer. They're great. Really, uh, interesting people."

For a moment, Liv faltered. If he thought Kiyoko was interesting, he probably thought Olivia was as exciting as a bowl of vanilla custard. Then she pulled herself together. *He asked you out,* she reminded herself. *He wanted to see you.* And she couldn't quite understand it—if someone asked for an explanation, she'd be at a complete loss for words—but the fact was that from the moment she'd met Eli, she felt connected to him in a way she didn't with most people. Most people probably thought she was fairly standoffish—the byproduct of being shy and somewhat uptight. But with Eli, she didn't feel judged at all, and just wanted to listen to him forever. With the possible intermittent hugging spell.

"If you don't mind me saying, I'm surprised that you and Kiyoko are such good friends," Eli said, breaking into Liv's warm, cozy thoughts. "You seem like polar opposites."

"I'm not bothered," Liv said. "You're quite right, you know. We are very different; she's much more

> **If he thought Kiyoko was interesting, he probably thought Olivia was as exciting as a bowl of vanilla custard.**

outgoing than I am, more extreme. In fact, we don't always get on so well," she admitted. "I reckon Kiyoko thinks I can be a bit of a prig. But . . . we have the internship, and we're both close with Alexa and Mel—two of the other interns. So all that keeps us together."

"Well, you know what they say: different strokes for different folks," Eli offered, raising his water glass and clinking it against Olivia's. "It takes all kinds."

"Do they really?" Olivia mused, smiling. "Who are these 'theys' I've been hearing so much about?"

Eli shook his head ruefully and dropped his voice to a conspiratorial whisper. "To be honest," he confessed, "I have no idea. But they do seem to know what they're talking about." He winked, and Olivia had to agree.

ᕰ ᕰ ᕰ ᕰ

"Now this place is very Kiyoko," Eli said, leading Liv down the street to a nondescript-looking bar.

"I don't even know what that means, really," Olivia protested.

"Me neither," Eli joked.

"And anyway, weren't we going to that hip-hop club?"

"We were, but now that my friend's not spinning tonight, it's not so much worth it. That place is dark and smoky. This place is dark, smoky, and *Latin*! In keeping with our theme for the night."

"But I thought bars in New York were smoke-free these days?" Olivia asked.

"Sure, but the better ones use smoke machines for atmospheric purposes," Eli said.

Olivia wasn't sure whether or not he was joking, but she laughed. "Brilliant."

He pushed the door open and led her inside. As promised, it was dark, smoky (well, more hazy, really, than anything else), and incredibly vibrant. In the corner, a salsa band played, and enthusiastic couples cut a path across the makeshift dance floor. The walls practically throbbed with energy.

"You do salsa, don't you?" Eli asked.

"Er, well . . . I'm quite adept at the waltz," Olivia replied, aware as the words came out of her mouth that she sounded like refugee from an Evelyn Waugh novel. "But I'm sure I can catch on."

"I have complete faith in you," he said. "Anyway, they're not strict here. You can just shake your hips and have a good time. No one expects you to get the steps perfectly."

"Excellent," she said.

"D'you want a caipirinha?" he asked, nodding his head in the direction of the bar.

"Well . . ." Olivia didn't want to seem like a killjoy, but they'd shared a little bit of sangria at dinner, and she

> ## 66 *She didn't fancy getting pissed on her first date.* 99

didn't fancy getting pissed on her first date. It wasn't especially classy. And, not to mention, she didn't want to get her photograph taken in that state.

"Yeah, I don't need anything, either," Eli said charmingly, letting her off the hook. He held out his arm to her tantalizingly. "Shall we?"

"We shall," she said, reaching out to him and clasping his hand. In a flash, they were weaving across the floor with the other couples. The movement was different than waltzing, absolutely, but Olivia didn't have any real problem keeping up. Eli laughed and smiled encouragingly at her as she faked her way through the more involved steps. She was grateful that Alexa had suggested she wear sexy-but-sensible flats for the night.

Going out with Eli is a bit of a walk on the wild side, Olivia realized as she whirled to and fro. Mind you, she fully recognized that there were plenty of girls who wouldn't exactly consider an evening in the East Village an adventure, but she couldn't help where she was from. She may not be as bold and daring as Kiyoko, but here she was, utterly enjoying herself with a boy she completely fancied, having a brilliant time. So this was a "Kiyoko" sort of place?

Well, she could live with that, for the night.

⟲　　⟲　　⟲　　⟲

At half-eleven, Liv forced herself to break away from Eli and lead him outside. "I'm so sorry to have to cut the evening short," she apologized.

"You're just getting back at me because of that time that I stomped on your toe."

She smiled. "If I'd a mind for revenge, it'd be in regard to the time that you tried to dip me—and nearly dropped me cold on the floor."

"See, I *knew* you were going to hold that against me!"

"Really, I'd love to stay out," Olivia went on, "but Emma was actually rather kind the other night when I missed curfew. So I'd prefer not to push my luck. She could have told Ms. Bishop about the whole incident. But instead, she kept the grounding just between us."

"I totally get it," Eli assured her. "My parents—when I'm home, that is—are weirdly protective of me. They're big into rules and regulations. Frankly, I was surprised that they were willing to let me go to school so far away."

Olivia found her thoughts wandering off, as she recalled how her own parents had first sent her to boarding school, when she was eight. No, the Bourne-

Cecils weren't into rules. Just appearances. She sighed. Eli seemed so down-to-earth, so normal. And from what he'd told her, he absolutely loved his parents. What would he think of her upbringing, a whirlwind of nannies and etiquette and jet-setting parents?

> **Eli seemed so down-to-earth, so normal.**

Nothing. He wouldn't think anything because he wouldn't ever find out. Eli was so interesting, so different than any boy she'd ever known, that she wouldn't risk revealing too much about herself and having him realize that they were, frankly, worlds apart.

"Besides," Eli was saying, oblivious to Liv's internal monologue, "I wouldn't want to get you in trouble with your housemother. After all, I can't have Emma mad at me if I'm going to be spending the rest of the summer getting to know you better, can I?"

"Well, I . . . um, suppose not . . ." Olivia faltered, pleased and embarrassed and shy all at once.

"Let's get you a cab," Eli suggested, eyes twinkling. He stepped into the street and held his hand up. Moments later, a yellow cab pulled smoothly to the curb in front of them. "Your chariot, milady," he said, opening the door for her with a flourish.

"Thank you, sir," Olivia giggled. She stepped forward, but Eli still had his arm on the inside of the

" How did one kiss a boy? "

door. Suddenly she was in very close proximity to his upper body. She could feel his breath on her cheek. Was he going to kiss her? She'd never properly kissed a boy before, with the exception of one ill-conceived game of spin-the-bottle in the hallway of a ninth-year dance. And that hardly counted, miserable as the experience had been. Her pulse quickened. How did one kiss a boy? Should she wait for him to lean in? Should she lean forward? Was kissing on the first date considered inappropriate? She had absolutely no clue. She vaguely recalled a conversation with an older cousin some years ago, in which closing one's eyes was discussed. Maybe she should close her eyes . . .

She was preparing to do a combination close-eyed lean-in when she felt it: Eli's lips brushing against her forehead softly, if only for an instant. She was relieved and disappointed all at once. "I had a great time, Olivia," he said, taking her face in his hands and gazing directly into her eyes.

"Me too," she said. "Thanks again."

"We'll do it again soon," he promised. He helped her into the cab and closed the door for her. "Get home safely," he called after her as the car pulled away.

"You too!" she said. He was too far away to hear

her by then, really just an ever-shrinking blot on the sidewalk in the distance, but no matter. It had been a perfect evening. Just perfect. Olivia had gotten in touch with her inner rebel. But better than that, she'd done it with Eli. As the cab careened to SoHo, Liv realized she was already counting the minutes until she'd be able to see him again.

chapter nine

HAUTE AND HEAVY

Heralding back to the days when Coco Chanel first established her classic label, couture has always been a means of expressing oneself through fashion. Back then, however, it was more about taking risks and being different, as opposed to today's pursuit of finding the exact perfect bag—that everyone else on the block is carrying.
[Delete]

s it turned out, Olivia didn't have to wait very long to see Eli again, after all. He called, as he promised he would, the very next day, and asked what she was doing on Sunday. She was free—or so she thought, until Mel reminded her that Trey had given the girls backstage passes to a rock show by one of the up-and-coming new indie rock bands that night. There was no way they were missing that. For starters, it was a professional semiobligation, and then second of all, Olivia wasn't the type to drop her mates just because a bloke she fancied happened to call.

"Oh, dear," Liv fretted. "I completely forgot about that. I'd invite him along, of course, but I haven't got an extra ticket."

"I think Kiyoko said she was covering something else tonight—a stand-up comedian or something," Mel offered. "I'm sure you could take her pass."

"Oh, take her free pass to go out on a date with her friend? Yes, I'm sure she'll love that. Not bloody likely. She's well possessive of Eli, you know," Liv said. She clapped her hands over her mouth, but it was too late; the words were out before she could stop them.

"Come on." Mel nudged her. "I mean, sure, you guys may be, like, total oil and water, but you should just cut her a break and hopefully she'll do the same. You're both good people. Wait, I know!" She beamed. "I'll get her pass from her—as long as you promise not to narc on me." She hesitated, biting her lip. "I hate to lie, but I really want you to come!"

"You'd do that for me?" Liv asked, somewhat incredulous. She was touched. Mel really wasn't the dishonest sort.

"Of course," Mel said, clearly resolved that this small deception was worthwhile. "I want you there; you want Eli there. It's a white lie. Enough said. No biggie."

◉   ◉   ◉   ◉

Mel did as she'd promised and came through in a huge way. Of course, Eli was quite excited to be invited along. Mel and Alexa dressed Liv for the concert, decking her out in low-rise distressed jeans and an adorable short-sleeved tee over a long-sleeved combo. They even flipped out the ends of her blond bob and secured the front with a bobby pin, against the tune of severe protests from Liv. "Honestly, I look like I'm twelve," she complained.

"Trust me, *chica*," Alexa said. "You do not look twelve." She looked Olivia up and down meaningfully, mock-leering at her. "Eli won't think so, either."

In the end, her friends won out, even going so far as to dig up a pair of hyper-trendy Prada trainers. "*Where* did these come from?" Liv gasped, marveling at the butter-soft leather.

"The Closet, duh," Mel said, rolling her eyes. "Jonah has been in a very generous mood lately. You're just lucky we wear the same size." One never knew when The Closet—a fashion mecca, *Flirt*-style—would be open to the interns. Obviously, at some point last week, Mel had scored. It was a double treat when the girls were allowed to keep what they found, which wasn't often.

◉   ◉   ◉   ◉

Olivia wasn't much for indie music—if and when she listened to music, it was generally of the sugar-spun pop variety—but she had to admit that the band was good. There was a certain appeal to the slim-hipped boys and their shaggy haircuts. They even dressed neopreppy, much like her extremely adorable date, Eli. For his part, Eli was suitably impressed to have garnered a backstage pass to the show. "I love being a VIP," he whispered to Olivia, pulling her hair back off her neck to speak directly into her ear and sending shivers down her spine. She nodded happily, far too blissed-out to form actual words. They watched the band perform from the front of the club, then shoved their way past the masses to meet up with the guys backstage.

"They're quite good, aren't they?" Liv asked.

"Huh?" He mocked not being able to hear her above the din, cocking one hand to his ear and looking puzzled. Olivia just laughed.

They shook all the band members' hands and smiled for a few photographers in between sets, then spent the rest of the night rehashing the show at a nearby diner. Olivia could tell that her friends were as smitten by Eli as she was, and the thought made her feel warm, glowy, proud, and excited all at once. The one drawback to the whole experience was that, on display as they were to all of her friends, she didn't get loads of private time with Eli. That was to say, no snogging. But it was okay. He was worth the wait.

ⓖ   ⓖ   ⓖ   ⓖ

The girls paid for their endless night the next

morning at *Flirt*, unfortunately. Liv stood over a lightbox, glancing at a contact sheet of some outtakes from the recent shoot. There was Tatyana Milova in her Big Bird costume—if only Liv's eyes weren't so tired and dry . . . she teetered a bit on her feet. This was dreadful. If Bishop were to come by . . .

"*Ai!* We need to get you some coffee, *ahora mismo*!" Alexa whispered, poking Liv in the ribs as she walked past her. "You look like death. What if Bishop catches you?"

"Trust me, I'm well aware," Olivia replied. "I've been downing caffeine all day. I even ate a handful of gummy bears for lunch, desperately hoping for a sugar rush. Fat lot of good it did me." She made a face. "All it did was make my tongue fuzzy, that."

"Hey, you're the lovesick wonder," Alexa pointed out. "And you seemed pretty happy to dodge curfew last night—which, speaking of, you're welcome," she said, referring to her willingness to scamper up the fire escape and check to ensure that the coast was clear. "You must *really* like him to risk getting grounded again."

Olivia turned bright red. "I suppose that's obvious, right? I do quite fancy him."

Alexa chuckled. "I love how your accent makes

66 *You look like death. What if Bishop catches you?* 99

everything sound all nice and polite. When really you're just dying to have a big fat snogfest with him, right?" she asked, borrowing Olivia's rather tongue-in-cheek phrase.

"You mind your manners," Olivia chided. "That's quite enough. Anyway, he's wonderful. I didn't think we had very much in common when we first met, but as it turns out, that hardly matters. We just—what does Mel say? 'Click.' " She held the contact sheet out to Alexa. "Speaking of clicking, brilliant job at the shoot. Lynne is sure to be pleased with your work. Have a look. The third one in of Tatyana is gorgeous."

Alexa complied and glanced at the sheet. "She's great, isn't she? She was so much fun at the shoot. Not like the usual parade of skeletons who wander through the office with their noses in the air."

"Yes, she's lovely," Olivia agreed. "And I don't think it's a put-on. She was at the skin-care launch that Gen took me to, and she recognized me. She was very friendly."

"Who was friendly, dear, hmm?"

Olivia looked up to see Bishop striding over to the girls purposefully. It wasn't uncommon for the publisher to make small talk with Olivia, since she was quite friendly with the Bourne-Cecils, but during business hours, she tended to be rather busy. Usually she saved her chitchat for first thing in the morning, or just at the end of the day, on her way out. Now she was stomping along like her legs were on fire, the crisp skirt of her wrap dress punctuating her movement like a metronome.

"Alexa and I were just talking about Tatyana Milova, the model," Olivia said. "She's always very decent to the interns, I reckon. She was with us."

Liv gestured to Alexa to jump into the conversation, but Alexa just stood stock-still, looking somewhat like a deer in headlights. Poor thing. Ms. Bishop could certainly be intimidating, that was for sure. If it weren't for their overlapping social circles, Olivia might be a bit shier, herself.

"Right, well," Bishop began, smiling tightly. "That's sweet. If very . . . particular. That is to say, we can't all be so accommodating of people who are not quite . . . how shall I say this . . . of our station."

A small peep of disbelief escaped from Alexa's lips, but she stifled it quickly, eyes wide.

"I'm not sure I know what you mean," Olivia said as politely as she possibly could. She had a sneaking suspicion that she knew *exactly* what Ms. Bishop meant, although she was certain she didn't want to.

"Let me be clear, then," Bishop said. She set a

> **"** *We can't all be so accommodating of people who are not quite . . . how shall I say this . . . of our station.* **"**

newspaper down on the table, next to the lightbox. It was opened to another photo from the gossip pages, just as incriminating as the shot of Olivia and Gen had been the other day. "This is your third foray in just as many weeks into 'Page Six,' is it not?"

Liv swallowed. There, front and center, was a blurry-but-still-identifiable shot of her—and Eli—holding hands and talking to the drummer of the band from the previous night's concert. The look on her face was unmistakable—she was thoroughly head-over-heels mad about Eli, who in turn looked rather like a reject from a hipster garage band. Which Liv suspected was the core of the current problem. "Yes, it seems to be," she said quietly, biting her lip.

> **Who in turn looked rather like a reject from a hipster garage band.**

"Olivia," Ms. Bishop said, leaning forward, "as a Bourne-Cecil, I'm sure you're no stranger to the public eye. But if that's so, then you must realize what a delicate position it is to be in."

"I suppose," Olivia hedged, very much disliking the direction that this conversation was taking.

"I know your parents fairly well, of course, and I'm quite certain I understand the caliber of person they

"Please, don't let's actually be having this conversation."

have in mind as far as your . . . 'gentlemen callers' are concerned."

Please, don't let's actually be having this conversation, Olivia thought, her stomach plummeting into the heels of her shoes. This was beyond awkward. She wanted to tell Ms. Bishop to stuff it, that her parents were overblown prats whose acutely honed sense of decorum had turned their daughter into an antisocial stuffed shirt. And that fortunately, Eli had somehow overlooked this glaring character flaw and given her a chance, anyway. And in the process drawn out a more laid-back, more open version of herself. Someone she liked and wanted to spend more time with.

But of course Liv couldn't say any of that. She could only stand stock-still, rooted to the ground as Bishop droned on about "appropriate mates" and "suitable social standing." It was like a nightmare. A very wordy, overly posh, snobby nightmare.

"Anyway, darling, the point is that I'm sure your parents have someone rather . . . *specific* for you in mind back home, and while you're here with me, I'd suggest that you not get too attached to any of these fly-by-night types."

"Oh, but Eli's not . . ." Alexa began, then trailed off when she realized the futility of this tack. Arguing for Eli's relative loyalty was most definitely not the way to go.

"I'm sure he's not," Bishop agreed, grinning and exposing sharp white teeth. "And yet." She turned on her razor-sharp heels and clipped off down the hall.

For a moment, neither girl said anything. The air was heavy and toxic.

"Phew," Alexa breathed, once Bishop was definitely out of earshot. "That is one tightly wound lady. Tell me your parents aren't like that."

"I'm afraid they are," Olivia said, barely daring to exhale herself. "I'm afraid they are."

⊙   ⊙   ⊙   ⊙

"So let me get this straight," Mel said, taking off the pair of oversize ghetto-fabulous sunglasses she was trying on and exchanging them for a Beatles-esque model. The long torturous day was *finally* over—Olivia had thought she was going to absolutely suffocate in that office—and the girls were strolling around SoHo, taking in the array of goods for sale on the sidewalks as well as in the myriad boutiques that studded the landscape. "Bishop actually lectured you on dating within your social class?" Mel's voice rose to a pitch that Olivia reckoned only dogs could hear.

"That's right," Olivia said. "Although she didn't exactly use those words." She slurped on her grande iced latte. She didn't care if four dollars wasn't truly cheap for a coffee—right now it was the only thing keeping her upright.

"The meaning was—how do you say—*implied*," Alexa chimed in.

"Good grief," Kiyoko weighed in, more on board with the whole romance thing now that Eli was like the Romeo to Olivia's Juliet. Amazing how it worked, that. But Olivia wasn't going to complain. Right now she needed all the support she could get.

"What do you think?" Mel asked about the sunglasses she had on.

"Those are cool," Olivia said. It was true. Most girls wouldn't be able to carry off John Lennon glasses, but somehow the featherweight frames just suited Mel's laid-back style.

"They're thirty dollars, though. Ridiculous," Mel said, replacing the glasses on the table they were surveying and starting to walk again.

> *My Guccis cost me at least a hundred quid.*

"Right? I mean—my Guccis cost me at least a hundred quid," Olivia said. After a moment, she realized that Mel had in fact meant the exact opposite—that thirty dollars was too much to spend on a pair of glasses on the street. She flushed. "But I suppose that's different," she finished lamely. For designer lenses, she thought one could expect to pay more. Though she had a feeling that Mel, dear Mel, would disagree.

"I suppose so," Mel teased, being diplomatic. "Anyway, I have to save my pennies. There's a purple skirt that's on sale at French Connection that I'm dying for."

"*Not* another big, poufy peasanty thing," Kiyoko groaned. "Lad, every time you add to your wardrobe, you end up buying the same old variation on your theme. Why even bother?"

"It's my own personal style," Mel said, laughing. "Stay out of it."

"It's a crying shame, that's what it is," Kiyoko retorted. She paused in front of the Rampage storefront, pointing at a red vinyl miniskirt. "I would pay you twenty dollars to wear that skirt to *Flirt*."

Mel rolled her eyes. "Obviously, the skirt costs at least fifty dollars. You could try to make this worth my while."

"All right, then," Kiyoko said, tapping her fingers

> *I would pay you twenty dollars to wear that skirt to Flirt.*

against her pink fringed shoulder bag. "London—*you* wear it."

"Why, I . . ." Olivia stopped in her tracks. As it happened, she couldn't quite come up with a very good reason why she shouldn't buy the skirt. She wasn't bothered spending a few quid on something fun and festive. At least, not in theory—though the contents of her wardrobe might suggest otherwise. No, that wasn't the problem. The problem was that she couldn't in a million years imagine herself wearing something like that. Her parents would think she'd gone mental. And they just might be right.

"You're stalling for time, Blondie," Kiyoko said, her voice taking on a slightly challenging edge.

It was true. But Liv wasn't keen on being called out on her hesitation. "I—"

The shrill, sharp buzz of her mobile sounded, rescuing her. "Saved by the bell," she said weakly. She looked at the caller ID—it was her mum. At 11 P.M. England time? Odd. "Hello?" she said, speaking tentatively into the receiver. The chances of this being good news were slim.

"Olivia! Thank goodness I've reached you!" her mother trilled, sounding breathless, ratcheting up Olivia's anxiety factor a few notches.

"Well, of course, Mummy, it's my mobile—I carry it with me at all times," she said.

"Right, dear. Well," she continued brusquely, obviously barely processing what Olivia was saying, "Josephine called me this afternoon. It seems she saw you in 'Page Six' again?" Her voice went up as though this were a question, when clearly it was not.

"Yes, we got to go backstage at a concert—isn't that brilliant! It's been wonderful interning at *Flirt*," Liv said, forging brightly forward before the inevitable ax could drop.

"It's not the concert that concerns me, dear, but rather the company that you're keeping. This boy in the picture, the one who's holding your hand? Am I to assume that you're romantically involved with him?"

"Well, we've only just begun dating, so it's not all that serious," Olivia protested, knowing as she spoke that her words were useless. She couldn't *believe* this— first Josephine Bishop, then her parents were coming down on her for dating Eli? When he was the first boy she'd ever properly dated *in her life*? And all because he hadn't been knighted by the queen. Ridiculous.

> **"Her parents were coming down on her for dating Eli? When he was the first boy she'd ever properly dated in her life? And all because he hadn't been knighted by the queen. Ridiculous."**

"You'd quite like him, I reckon," Liv ventured.

Her mother laughed a sharp, brittle cackle. "Seems unlikely. In any event, I'm sure JoJo took time out of her *extremely* busy day to speak to you about the appropriateness of dating someone like that. Or rather, the inappropriateness."

"Someone who wears trainers out in public?"

"Don't get smart with me, young lady, but yes. Exactly. Obviously, I don't know that"—she sniffed—"*boy* very well, but your father and I have some lovely young men for you to meet when you come home."

"Absolutely, Mother. I look forward to it. Only three weeks left," Olivia said brightly, feeling a pang in the pit of her stomach already. Whatever would she do without Mel, Alexa—even Kiyoko, Gen, and Charlotte? She'd only just learned to do the washing up last week— summer couldn't be ending so quickly!

And Eli. No matter what her mother or anyone else said, she would miss Eli terribly.

"You're missing the point, Olivia," her mother said, overenunciating the syllables of her name in such a way that Liv knew the woman meant business. "You're to come home immediately. Your father and I discussed it with Josephine, and she understands. She won't hold it against you, and you can return to *Flirt* next summer if your father and I agree that you're ready. It's not just the boy, not at all. Remember, you were in hot water with JoJo back when she discovered that your friend had set up that website—"

"—blog," Olivia interjected, knowing full well that it was futile.

"Then you were caught on camera drinking at the art gallery. Then we read in the gossip pages that you and a friend are right pissed at a sponsor party, and now this boy? You seem to have taken complete leave of your senses. And your father and I just won't stand for it. We've decided: You are to come home. Immediately," she repeated, her tone stony and firm.

You are to come home. Immediately.

It was like the air had suddenly been sucked out of the atmosphere; Olivia's breath came in short, ragged gasps. She felt woozy, like she might faint. "Pardon?" she asked, her voice barely a whisper. She clutched the mobile to her chin to avoid dropping it completely.

"Well, obviously you're completely out of control," her mother said. "The situation with that website was absurd."

"Blog," Olivia corrected again, thinking back to Alexa's masterpiece. They'd all been somewhat implicated in that debacle, regardless of who had first launched the blog. It wasn't really worth protesting.

"Then the photo with your friend drunk—I've

seen those shows on the entertainment channel, you know. We do have Sky, dear."

Olivia really had nothing to say to that. It was pointless to try to convince her mother that it had been Gen who had been reenacting a hostess from "Wild On" rather than herself. Clearly, it was all the same to her parents. Liv's own mistake had been allowing herself to be photographed.

"And now this," her mother finished, her tone dire. "Your father and I discussed it, and you're to come home immediately."

"Mum, I simply can't. I won't," Olivia said, surprising herself. She'd never spoken to her parents so boldly before in her life. It was downright rude, it was. And she didn't even care. She looked up to see Kiyoko, Alexa, and Mel pumping their fists and giving one another high fives. Even if they weren't sure what Liv and her mum were talking about, they got the general idea. And they had her back. It was a great feeling. If only it had come under slightly less anxiety-provoking circumstances.

A moment of clarity washed over Olivia, stronger than ever. Since she'd come to New York, she'd gone to parties in the outer boroughs, taken the subway, and learned to use a washing machine (well, in theory, even though she'd rinsed her cashmere pants out by hand)—small points for most girls, but right triumphant

> **You want your independence? Well, I think you'll be quite surprised to find that you've got it.**

moments for her. And she had three weeks left. Three weeks to exercise her newfound independence. She wasn't about to let that go.

Not to mention, she still had to wow Ms. Bishop and Demetria with a knock-'em-dead sidebar for the haute couture issue.

"I'm sorry, Mum, I don't mean to be impolite, but I'm really learning loads here—more than you can imagine—and I just don't think it makes sense to go home right now. I'll behave, I swear"—though she had no idea how exactly she was going to be on any better behavior than she already was—"and I'll make you both proud, you'll see. I'm even meant to have a piece published in the actual magazine. But I won't come home just now. I can't." She paused to take a breath. She had absolutely no idea what her mum would say. She'd probably go mental, as a matter of fact. For her part, Olivia's heart was hammering against the inside of her rib cage. She didn't think she'd ever spoken up to her mother quite like this before. And she wasn't completely sure how she'd summoned the nerve to do so now. Maybe her parents would simply lock her up in another Swiss boarding school from now until she was thirty-five.

But to Olivia's surprise, when her mother spoke again, it was with a slow, measured calm. "All right, Olivia," she said, overenunciating Liv's name again. "If you insist, I can't exactly force you. Or, rather, I suppose I could, but I don't think it would do either of us a bit of good. So go ahead, stay the summer out. You want your independence? Well, I think you'll be quite surprised to find that you've got it."

The line went dead. Olivia stared at the phone in her hand, mouth agape.

Alexa was the first to break the silence, whooping excitedly. "You sure told her, *muchacha*!" she shrieked. "We're free! Now, we party!"

"Absolutely," Olivia said uncertainly. She looked at her phone quizzically, then stashed it back in her bag. "It'll be brilliant." She tried to force a smile to her face.

Deep down, though, she wasn't a bit convinced that the next three weeks would be brilliant—not at all. Her mother wasn't exactly a pushover, and this was one argument she'd given up far too easily. Olivia had a sneaking suspicion that her mother's plans for her independence might be . . . complicated. And that there might be some surprises waiting around the bend.

Liv had no idea what to expect. Which meant that there was no way to be ready. None at all.

chapter ten

From: flyguy@hh.net
To: liv_b-c@flirt.com
Subject: 2night

U free? I think I'm going into withdrawal. It's been forty-eight whole hours, after all . . . Maybe a burger or something?

—Eli

P.S. Did you catch that pic of us in "Page Six"? Bizarre! My roommate showed it to me. I guess we're famous or something . . .

. . . .

From: liv_b-c@flirt.com
To: flyguy@hh.net
Subject: Re: 2night

Withdrawal? That's no good. Well, they say that the

first step is admitting that you have a problem.

Tonight would be great. I should finish up here around half-six. Have to go work on some caption copy. Call me on my mobile when you've got a plan. Burgers or anything else . . .

—Liv

P.S. Could really fancy a curry, tho. Just a thought.

P.P.S. I did see the photo. It is strange! I reckon it's not that we're famous, tho. I think the photo had to do with the popularity of the band. I can't think of any other reason why we'd be captured on film for posterity. Can you?

. . . .

"You realize, of course, that you're killing me with that accent. No exaggeration. You could ask me anything and I'd be putty in your hands."

"Anything? Really? Well, that bears some more thought," Olivia said, laughing and reaching across the dinner table to take Eli's hand.

The two of them were on East Sixth Street, in the area known as Little India. As Liv had walked down the street with Eli, she'd been overwhelmed by the smells of curry and other Indian spices. Not to mention the restaurateurs who stood in front of their shoe-box-size eateries, calling to passersby and beckoning them to come inside to try their delectable food.

"I can't tell you how excited I am that you introduced me to this neighborhood," Olivia continued, still holding Eli's hand. "A good curry is something I miss dreadfully from back home. We used to have it on Thursday nights," she explained, "to give the cook a break, you know? I was so homesick for it when I got here."

"I can't believe no one told you about Little India," Eli said, incredulous. "I also sort of can't believe you have a cook."

Oh, sod it. And here she'd been trying to downplay her social standing with Eli. Talking to Eli made Olivia feel comfortable and open. Which made this whole dishonesty thing that much more difficult. "Yes, yes, I'm quite posh," Olivia semijoked, trying to recover. "She's really just, you know, a cleaner who comes in to

" Yes, yes, I'm quite posh. "

help my mother once in a while." Was he buying this? She couldn't tell. She forged onward, clumsily changing the subject. "Well, it's taking me some time to get to know Manhattan. And it has taken me a while to get to know my flatmates, as well," Olivia admitted. "These days, we're much closer. But still very different."

"Like you and I," he commented, eyes twinkling.

"Yes," Olivia said, flustered. She pulled her hand back to her side of the table nervously.

"I'm sorry, but can we go back to the cook thing?" Eli asked, reading her edginess and wisely lightening the mood with a joke, albeit one couched in sincerity. "Very . . . *posh*," he said, borrowing her phrase.

Olivia laughed nervously. "I suppose so, although you get used to anything when it's all you know. Besides, lots of people in London have cooks. It's quite normal." This wasn't strictly true. She squirmed uncomfortably in her seat. "The truth is, I'd be just as happy with one of those American-style working mums, who are always running around in chaos, ordering pizzas for supper every night."

"You'd never see her, then," Eli pointed out.

"Oh, I never see my mum, anyway," Olivia said breezily. "She's off most nights . . . well, she volunteers quite a bit," she finished lamely. Her voice caught slightly and she coughed, then reached for her water.

"Have you decided what you're going to order?" she asked, turning to regard the menu in front of her and brightly changing the subject. How was it that Eli was drawing her to so many of her touchier subjects? She wanted to open up to him, but she wasn't sure she was ready yet. And this was the first time a boy liked her for *her*, not for who her family was. And she was liking it. "I think we should get at least one order of naan," Liv suggested, referring to the chewy bread that was a staple at most Indian meals.

"Definitely. Naan, check," Eli said. "In fact, why don't you choose what we eat tonight? You're the expert, coming from jolly old England. I'm in your hands." He paused, smiling. "Wait, I didn't mean it like that."

"Cheeky," Olivia said, shaking her head. "Well, as long as you trust me." There was double meaning to the words, she realized. But she wasn't ready to say anything more.

"Oh, I do," Eli assured her. "I completely and totally do."

⟲   ⟲   ⟲   ⟲

Two hours later, the remains of the meal lay strewn across the table before them: rich, creamy *sag paneer*, or spinach with cheese; and *aloo gobi*, a chickpea-and-potato mixture drenched in delicate tomato sauce. And of course, Olivia's personal favorite, lamb *rogan josh*, prepared in heavy tomato, onion, and cream sauce.

"Right, then," she said, laughing. "I'm stuffed. I reckon I won't eat for at least a week." She patted her stomach contentedly.

"Famous last words, girl," Eli said. "I've seen you

pack it away. I give you three hours, tops, before you start jonesing for the sour apple gummy candy again."

"How did you . . . ?" she started, then remembered that she almost always had a half-eaten bag of the stuff in her handbag at any given time. It wouldn't take a rocket scientist to put two and two together. "Actually, the fizzy colas are my favorite," she confessed. She giggled.

She loved that Eli already knew her vice: sugary candy. She loved that he thought it was odd, as opposed to a given, that her parents' household back in London had a cook, among other servants and waitstaff. That was normal for everyone she knew back home. Funnily enough, that hadn't bothered her then—when she'd been home. Since coming to New York City, she was finally starting to meet a more diverse, eclectic group of people. It was why she had come, and she loved it, just as she loved so many things about Eli. She loved that she had confided in him about the fact that her

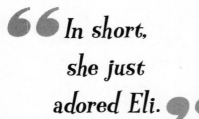**In short, she just adored Eli.**

parents weren't around all that often, and that when that topic had proven to be a bit too emotional, he'd deftly and sensitively allowed her to change the subject. In short, she just adored Eli. She thought it was wonderful the way that he embraced their differences. And more so, the way that she felt comfortable talking to him about almost

> ## What sort of sixteen-year-old only went on preapproved dates with preapproved suitors?

anything. And she was warming up more to him as the days passed.

She frowned. She was opening up to him about anything and everything—except for the truth about her pedigree. And she hadn't told him about her sidebar, or the lack of it. It was due imminently, and she'd yet to come up with anything cool, edgy, or even remotely worthwhile to write about. She thought about asking Eli's advice—he was dead trendy (in the best possible way), after all—but she was terrified of admitting to him that dating him was the "wildest" thing she'd ever done. Going out with someone who wasn't a member of British high society? That was Olivia, rocking out. So lame. And no matter how understanding and open Eli was, he was sure to be skeptical of that fact. What sort of sixteen-year-old only went on preapproved dates with preapproved suitors?

The ridiculous, shy, immature sort. Or so she reckoned.

"Should we get the check?" Eli asked, breaking into her thoughts.

"What? Oh, quite right," Olivia said. She straightened up in her seat, taking in the disco-party vibe of the small, cramped, and informal room: crepe-paper streamers hung from the walls and psychedelic Bollywood dance music thumped from oversize speakers placed strategically along the corners of the dining area. "But this one's on me. I insist."

"No way. You gave me that backstage pass to that concert. I owe you," Eli reminded her, reaching into his back pocket to retrieve his wallet.

Oh, right. That. But . . . somewhere, somehow, there was a flaw in this logic. She thought for a moment. *There* it was.

"No, Eli, sorry. That was free from *Flirt*, so it doesn't count." She folded her arms across her chest imposingly. "I'm a modern woman, Eli, and I won't be waited on hand and foot." *Not this Bourne-Cecil, anyhow,* she thought, the very idea making her mouth turn up at the corners. Her parents would go absolutely mental to hear their little Olivia say such a thing.

"Well, I'd hate to interfere with the progress of the feminist movement," Eli said uncertainly. "Just so long as you let me get the next one."

Olivia nodded. "You can also be 'the boy' and ask for the check."

Eli winked. "That I can do." He flagged down their waiter and indicated that they were ready. Moments later, the bill was placed on the table in a faux-leather fold—just in front of Eli, of course. Typical.

"Minus two points for the progress of the feminist movement," Olivia quipped. "Of course he set it right down in front of you without even asking."

> **Minus two points for the progress of the feminist movement.**

"Don't go burning your bra just yet," Eli implored her, sliding the check across the table toward her.

She plunked her credit card down on top of the bill, and the waiter magically reappeared to whisk it away. Olivia took the moment to savor the funky tunes, the spicy, heady scents wafting through the restaurant, and, of course, her date's fine bone structure. Was this going to be the night that he finally kissed her for real? They'd been getting bolder about the hand-holding and other gestures of affection, but really, it was hardly the same thing. Maybe she should just take matters into her own hands. *Or my own lips, as it were,* she mused. But no. That just might be taking the progress of the feminist movement a bit too far.

Still, though, he was so cute. Right fit, tall, and with a brilliant smile . . .

"Sir, I'm sorry," the waiter said, shattering Olivia's reverie by plunking the bill right back down—in front of Eli yet again, naturally. "I'm sorry, but your card has been declined."

"But that's—impossible," Olivia gasped. Her parents paid the balance of the bill off every month; she never even saw the bills. Clearly, there was a mistake here of sorts. How embarrassing.

"I'm sorry," the waiter repeated, apparently feeling awful about being the bearer of such relatively humiliating news. He lowered his voice so as not to broadcast her shame to the entire restaurant. "We did run it through three times. It is not working. Perhaps you should call the credit card company?" He looked at Eli.

"Yes, well, it's actually mine," Olivia said, deeply flustered and blushing furiously. She snatched the card back and thrust it into her wallet. How could this be? Surely there was a misunderstanding with the credit card company. Idiots.

"No problem," Eli said smoothly, reaching for his wallet once again. "I've got it." To Olivia's look of consternation, he insisted, "You can get me back next time. Seriously."

She didn't fancy making a bigger scene than they already had—obviously, the waiter, despite his commendable manners, thought they were children or otherwise unreliable—so she agreed numbly. She'd have to call the bank immediately. Or her parents—

> ❝ *Her parents. They'd done this.*
> *They must have. What else*
> *could it possibly be?* ❞

She stopped, the realization hitting her like a ten-stone weight. Her *parents*.

They'd done this. They must have. What else could it possibly be?

This was what her mother had meant when she'd told Olivia she was going to be independent from now on. This was the shocking outcome of that cryptic conversation. This was why she had agreed to let Olivia stay in the States and forge her own way. They'd closed off her credit accounts.

They'd cut her off.

Olivia had wanted a crash course in autonomy, that was true. And it looked like she was going to get what she'd asked for.

And then some.

chapter eleven

From: liv_b-c@flirt.com
To: mtbourne-cecil@runner.uk
Subject: A small problem

Hello, Father and Mum:

How are you? I do hope that all is well at the Manor, and that you've gotten in some good riding over the course of the summer despite your hectic schedules! Ms. Bishop showed me the clipping from the Harrod's auction; looks like you had a brilliant turnout. (I should add, Mum, that your dress was absolutely gorgeous. Marc Jacobs, no?)

I'm having a wonderful time at Flirt and am learning quite a lot. Ms. Bishop has kept an eye out for me (though of course, there's been no preferential treatment!). My flatmates are great, too, and being in New York City is very exciting. I'll have some lovely photos to show you when I come home—in just three weeks! Will you be around, or will you have left for Mauritius by then? It's so difficult to keep your schedules straight. I haven't had a chance to ask the housekeeper if she's keeping your diary, so I thought I'd go straight to the source, for once!

I did actually have one question for you, and it's somewhat of a difficult question to address, so please do bear with me: The other night while I was out to dinner with some friends, I had the rather embarrassing experience of some credit card trouble. That is to say that my card was declined. At first I thought it was surely a mistake, but the waiter ran it through several times, after which point he took two of my other cards and tried the same thing.

Needless to say that if it was a mistake, in fact it was a rather pervasive error. So I can't help but wonder whether or not the two of you know something about this?

Mum, I know we discussed the appropriateness of the company I've been keeping this summer, and there's been some question of my behaviour on a variety of occasions. I can't help but feel, however, that if in fact the two of you have chosen to cut me off, that your decision has been rather a hasty one.

I can't quite fathom how to convince you to trust me just a little bit more. Being in New York City on my own has been absolutely fantastic. And while I've branched away from the type of people that we tend to spend our time with at home, I can't say I think there's anything wrong with that. For my part, I have to say that I feel I am learning quite a bit about myself through this experience—and that's exciting!

Well, I certainly didn't mean to go on for this long; I'm sure I've made my point and then some. But I would love the chance to talk about this with the two of you further. It's not the money so much as the lack of trust. I'm sure that you have your reasons for doing what you've done, but I would really like to discuss this more fully, if you don't mind. Just let me know what you think.

Best,

Olivia

P.S. Please pet Fergie for me and give her a treat. I reckon she's confused as to where I've gone off to. The last time we were separated for this long was when we all went on holiday to Greece over Christmas, and that was when I was eight years old!

(Delete)

"Your parents did *what*?!" Alexa shrieked. Alexa, it would seem, was rather prone to shrieking, regardless of the shriekworthiness of the event in question.

"Well, they cut me off," Olivia said glumly. "They thought I was asserting too much independence. Or misbehaving. Or keeping the wrong kind of company. To be honest, I'm not totally certain. I suppose it was all of those things. "

"And that's bad? Independence?" Kiyoko asked, downright incredulous. She slumped back in her seat and folded her arms across her chest, fuming.

When Olivia had come home from her date with Eli, the loft had been mercifully empty. Mel, Kiyoko, and Alexa were off seeing the latest romantic comedy, and Gen and Charlotte were taking a private Pilates class courtesy of the health and fitness beat at *Flirt*. She hadn't minded, though; the privacy afforded her a chance to collect her thoughts about the evening's horrible turn of events.

Eli had been wonderfully gracious about the credit card debacle, which was lovely. He hadn't minded getting the check, and also rather politely avoided pointing out the obvious crux of the situation: that her parents had cut her off, full stop. Another massive relief; the last thing Liv was prepared to do was to somehow explain to Eli just why, exactly, her parents would do such a thing. Considering he was a prime motivating factor for them . . .

So she'd come home and composed about six different e-mails to her parents, each of which she ultimately deleted. It was too awkward, too delicate of a situation. In the end, she'd simply broken down and called her father on his mobile, a terrifying prospect under even the most ideal circumstances. He'd answered her on the second ring, gruffly informing her that he was "rather in the middle of something."

When she'd timidly suggested that perhaps her parents had something to do with this recent turn of financial events, he had confirmed the theory, thereby solidifying her very worst nightmares. "You have your bank account—the money we set aside for the internship—and you can live off of that for the rest of the summer. It's not what you're used to, but you can manage on it," he informed her. "Or you can come home. Your choice."

"It was a right rotten choice, that's what it was."

It was a right rotten choice, that's what it was. But there was no question in her mind what she was going to do—for better or for worse.

Once the girls returned to the loft, Olivia filled them in on the situation. Everyone agreed that it was nothing short of a major crisis, and they headed out to debrief at the corner coffee shop. Now Olivia sat back on a plush overstuffed couch, glumly stirring a skim latte and giving her mates the full lowdown of the sorry state of affairs.

"With my parents, yes, independence is not great," she said. "Neither is, apparently, public drunkenness or dating someone who is not a member of the royal family." It was an exaggeration, but not by that much.

She took a sip of her coffee, found it lukewarm, grimaced, and placed it back onto the table in front of her. Three dollars, essentially just chucked in the bin, and all for a subpar coffee. She'd have to start considering her purchases quite a bit more carefully if she was to somehow stretch her budget through the last three weeks of the internship. "Really, anything that goes against their ideas of what would be proper is B-A-D.

If I had to guess, declining an invitation from that daft Phoebe Winters was my first mistake."

"No, your first mistake was letting Gen Tara Reid her way into 'Page Six' at that makeup party—and implicate you in the process," Mel offered helpfully. She was fuming, brimming over with sympathetic, righteous indignation. If only the situation hadn't been so dire, Olivia might have found it quite touching.

"That's not the point," Olivia said, deftly steering her friends back to the real heart of the matter. "The problem is that I don't have all that much in my bank account, New York City being as expensive as it is. And I'm certainly not going home to England early. Not after all this. What'd be the point? I may as well stick it out—prove something to myself and to them." She sighed. The whole situation felt quite futile and overwhelming. She wasn't accustomed to being overwhelmed. As a general rule, life for Olivia was rather well-regimented and therefore quite under control at all times.

"*Ai, sí,* but what will you do?" Alexa asked, stating the very blatant, obvious question. She twirled her thick brown hair around her index finger furiously, looking

❝ *Your first mistake was letting Gen Tara Reid her way into 'Page Six' at that makeup party.* ❞

rather worried. *It is sweet, the concern my friends are showing,* Olivia thought.

"What do people do when they need money?" Olivia asked. "They get jobs." She'd given this a lot of thought and didn't really see any way around it. She'd never held a job proper—the *Flirt* internship being unpaid—but she'd done loads of volunteer work. Somehow that experience had to translate. She was smart, she knew, and a hard worker. That had to count for something.

> **She was smart, she knew, and a hard worker.**

Too bad she had absolutely no idea how one went about getting a job.

Not to mention, the citizenship thing could be a problem. She had a work visa that *Flirt* had arranged for her as part of the internship, but it only covered her time at the magazine—not employment anywhere else.

"We're at the magazine from nine to six every day," Mel pointed out. Liv knew she wasn't trying to be negative, but rather just realistic. "It's probably going to be hard to hold down a job at the same time."

Liv shrugged. "What choice do I have?" She looked sheepishly around the table at her friends' supportive faces. "The thing is, though, I don't really know how one goes about getting a job. Or what types of jobs would pay a reasonable amount. Or what sort of jobs are available, you know, outside of regular business hours. I suppose bartending? Waitressing? Do they hire people our age to be waitresses in New York City?" She tapped her perfect manicure on the table in frustration, then ceased abruptly when she realized that it might be her last manicure for quite some time, and therefore should be preserved at all costs.

"You seem serious about this," Kiyoko said, a grudging admiration tingeing her tone. "The whole 'working' thing."

"I am," Olivia said, thrusting her chin out somewhat defiantly. For some reason, she truly felt that she had something to prove—perhaps not to Kiyoko, or even to her parents. But to herself.

"Well, if that's the case, lad," Kiyoko said, leaning forward conspiratorially, "I just may be able to help you out."

> **"** *She tapped her perfect manicure on the table in frustration, then ceased abruptly when she realized that it might be her last manicure for quite some time, and therefore should be preserved at all costs.* **"**

chapter twelve

"**Y**es, it's brilliant—a friend of Kiyoko's works at a restaurant, and one of the waitresses just quit last week, completely out of the blue. So they're looking to hire, and Kiyoko says that if she puts in a good word for me, I shouldn't have a problem getting the job. Voilà! Problem solved." Olivia laughed over the phone line to Eli, whom she was bringing up to speed on the events that had transpired since their fateful dinner.

"Well, *one* of your problems solved," Eli said cautiously. "Babe, you know I totally support you, and I think it's great that you're doing things on your own, and on your terms, but . . . waiting tables is really hard work."

"You think I can't do it?" Olivia asked, slightly stung.

"I most definitely think that you, my dear, can do anything you put your mind to. But you do have the internship, which takes up a lot of your time. And waitressing is grueling. You're on your feet all night."

"It's not as though I've *never* worked," Olivia protested, slightly sulky. "Last year my mum and I helped plan a food drive in conjunction with some friends of hers at B Sky B."

"Okay, point taken," Eli said. "And I'm sure that was not

> ## " Well, London, I have to confess, I do admire your can-do attitude. "

exactly a walk in Hyde Park . . . but how many actual, paying jobs have you ever had?"

"Zero," Olivia grumbled reluctantly. "Zip. Zed." She forced herself to be brighter. "But there's a first time for everything!" Ironically enough, her parents had certainly not taught her to be a quitter.

Even Eli had to chuckle at this. "Well, London, I have to confess, I do admire your can-do attitude. And I've completely got your back."

That's perfect, Olivia thought, though she kept her feelings to herself, at least for now. "That's all I need from you," Olivia chirped. "And the truth is that of course I appreciate your concern. I'm sure there will be a bit of a learning curve here. Perhaps more than a bit."

"My older sister waited tables one summer out in Nantucket," Eli said. "So I have one pearl of wisdom to pass along."

"What's that?" Olivia asked, genuinely curious.

"Wear flats," he recommended. "For real."

Olivia giggled, but his well-intentioned advice made its intended impact.

What was she getting herself into?

◉　　◉　　◉　　◉

Olivia made her way down the crumbly pavement of Astor Place, clutching a crumpled Post-it note upon which Kiyoko had scrawled an address: *Moe's, 312 Astor btwn 2nd and 3rd.*

Moe's was a restaurant where a friend of Kiyoko's worked, and as Kiyoko had explained, they were hiring. As Olivia had told Eli, one of their waitresses had quit at rather an inopportune time, and therefore they weren't being terribly fussy about who they interviewed. They were strapped, understaffed, after all, and evidently open twenty-four hours a day. And meanwhile, Kiyoko had called and put in a good word for Olivia. So Olivia had been called down on her lunch hour to interview with the manager.

Which might, she fretted inwardly, *go straight into the bin when they realize how dreadfully underqualified I am.*

No, underqualified is being generous. I've no experience in this sort of thing whatsoever.

Olivia really had no idea how her parents would feel about her working in a twenty-four-hour joint called Moe's. Or rather, she had some idea, she just chose not to dwell upon it. Working at Moe's—or even considering working at Moe's—was probably somewhat on par to declining a social invite from the illustrious Phoebe

66 *Restaurant was evidently a generous term for this establishment.* **99**

Winters. *Simply not done, dear,* Olivia thought, her mother's voice echoing in her head.

308, 310 . . . 312. This was . . . it?

Oh, dear.

Restaurant was evidently a generous term for this establishment. Moe's was a twenty-four-hour dive in the great tradition of all-night diners, set apart perhaps only by a small claim stamped in faded white on the threadbare awning: We Serve Organic.

Organic what? Olivia thought wildly. *No, best not to dwell.*

She pushed the front door open, taking care not to flinch when its hinged squeaked. It slammed shut against the door frame with a clang that startled her. Though Moe's was open twenty-four hours a day, at 1 P.M. on a Wednesday—Olivia had done her best to slip away from Demetria at lunchtime—it was relatively deserted. The Formica tables were chipped. The lighting was dim, but not in a romantic sense. A giant ceiling fan oscillated lazily overhead, stirring the humid air into great circles. Moe's was clearly a local hangout, a place for college students to grab a cheap pint and maybe some chips.

Organic chips, at that.

"Can I help you?" A skinny, petite girl whose

forearms crawled with tattoos emerged from somewhere behind the bar. Her hair was an inky, unnatural black and stood up in sharp spikes around her head. Her eye makeup was dark

> *Olivia was impressed by this tiny girl, and also slightly afraid of her.*

and sooty. Olivia was impressed by this tiny girl, and also slightly afraid of her.

"Yes, I'm here to speak to"—she glanced at her crumpled piece of paper—"Miguel? I'm a friend of Kiyoko's."

"Sure," the girl said, shrugging. She clearly had no idea who Kiyoko was and couldn't care less. "He's in the back."

She wandered off toward the ambiguous "back," narrow hips swaying in her wake. Her thick-soled black shoes made clomping noises against the uneven wood floor. Olivia wasn't certain whether she was supposed to follow this girl—she really hadn't made any such intimations, after all—so instead Liv stood still, rooted to the ground, waiting for Miguel to emerge, her terror increasing in mild increments as the moments ticked by.

After what felt like an eternity but was probably more like five minutes, a stocky, balding man with a deep tan and leathery skin surfaced. "Can I help you?"

he asked gruffly. He wiped the back of his hand against his nose and Olivia had to physically restrain herself from shuddering.

"Yes, my friend Kiyoko Katsuda mentioned that you were hiring?" Olivia said, forcing a bright smile on her face.

Miguel frowned. "She works here?"

"No, her friend . . . Stasia . . . is a waitress here, I believe," Olivia said. Inwardly, she panicked. Hadn't Kiyoko spoken to Stasia? Hadn't Stasia spoken to Miguel? This breakdown in communication could be the beginning and end of her financial independence.

"Oh, yeah! She mentioned you were comin' in," Miguel said, perking up considerably at the spark of recognition. "So, you got experience?"

"I've . . . hosted some charity dinners," Olivia hedged, hoping he wouldn't ask for a more specific description of the like.

"References?"

"Well, they're in England, but certainly."

He looked baffled by the thought of making a long-distance call. He scratched his chin. "Well, today's Wednesday."

Olivia nodded, unsure whether or not she was expected to further comment on this observation.

"Can you work tomorrow evening?"

She thought quickly. Tomorrow she was

supposed to see a film with Melanie—the romantic comedy with the perky blonde and the "Sexiest Man Alive" (according to certainly weekly magazines). Supposedly they were shagging in real life, and they had loads of onscreen chemistry.

But.

He was essentially offering her the job. A job she really had no business being hired for, woefully unqualified as she was. So she should take it. She had connections in this city, after all, but none in this type of environment. Kiyoko was going out on a limb, helping her out this way. It wasn't like her, really, and it wasn't especially likely to happen again. Olivia glanced furtively at the scuffed wooden floors, the scratched Formica tables, the salt-and-pepper shakers thick with crust that sat on the surface of the bar. Could she work tomorrow?

"Certainly."

From: liv_b-c@flirt.com
To: kiyoko_k@flirt.com
Subject: You're brilliant!

Truly and completely! I got the job! I can't thank you enough. Cross your fingers for me that I don't manage to make too much of a mess of things.

See you back at the loft!

—Olivia

. . . .

From: kiyoko_k@flirt.com
To: liv_b-c@flirt.com
Subject: Flattery will get you everywhere . . .

You're welcome. Glad I could be of service. I'm sure you'll be awesome tomorrow. Just, you know, don't spill anything or screw up anyone's tab and you'll be A-OK, lad.

—K

P.S. Wear flats. Seriously.

. . . .

From: liv_b-c@flirt.com
To: flyguy@hh.net
Subject: May I take your order?

I start tomorrow!

. . . .

From: flyguy@hh.net
To: liv_b-c@flirt.com
Subject: !!!

Awesome! Though I must say, I never once doubted your powers. I can't wait to hear all about it. Moe's, huh? I hear they serve organic. But, organic what?

Best not to dwell, right?

. . . .

ⓖ　　ⓖ　　ⓖ　　ⓖ

"Table thirteen, order up!"

"Liv, that's you!"

"What? Oh . . ." Liv whirled around to see Ingrid, the sullen-looking girl who'd greeted Liv yesterday for her interview, looking even more sullen than she had then, if that was even possible. Ingrid jerked her head in the direction of the window to the kitchen. "Table thirteen," she hissed. "That's your section. And they're going to be really pissed if their food is cold."

"Right, of course," Liv said, blowing a wisp of hair out of her eyes and reaching out to grab the platter from the counter. *Table thirteen. Now, which one was that?* She looked out at the dining area and tried to count successively, clockwise from the front door. She was guessing, at best, but she'd rather die than ask Ingrid for any more help. The girl was about as warm as a sudden winter hailstorm. *You'd think she'd be grateful for the extra help,* Liv thought to herself. Deep down, though, Liv suspected that she might be getting in the way more than anything else.

So far, on this shift, she'd switched two orders, gotten three of them mixed up, and brought one couple on a first date the wrong check. She would have thought, maybe, that they'd think this was funny, being in the first flush of romance and all that, but no such luck. Liv reckoned that the boy was mostly embarrassed at having to call out the minute details of his bill. His dissatisfaction had been reflected in his tip, as well. Olivia vowed several hours ago never to tip less than 25 percent for any service.

There, by the window. Those people look impatient. They must be table thirteen. The one man was tapping at the table like an overcaffeinated Jack Russell terrier. She wove her way toward them, taking care not to get in Ingrid's way in the process.

"Let's see, now, I've got your meals ready," she

> **The girl was about as warm as a sudden winter hailstorm.**

chirped, glancing back down at the tray. A soy burger platter, a sprout salad, and a hummus sandwich. It was all she could do not to flinch. The "organic" question had been answered—and she almost wished that it hadn't been, at that. She looked back at the three expectant faces.

And drew a blank.

She had no idea which meal belonged to whom. She checked her tray to see if she'd written it down on the check. No such luck. She was going to have to confess to being utterly daft and forgetful.

"Who had the soy burger?"

The impatient man scowled at her and indicated that it was his. She placed it down on the table before him.

"That's mine," a woman—either his date or his wife—said, pointing at the salad. *She looks like the type who'd eat a sprout salad,* Olivia thought. The woman's face was tight and pinched, and her cheekbones were as sharp as icicles.

"Well then," Olivia said, grinning, "this must be yours." She made a big show of leaning forward to pass the hummus to the third member of their party, a disaffected-looking preteen who was clearly trying very hard not to pay anyone any mind at all. Confidently, Olivia slid the heavy plate down. In fact, she was so confident with her gesture that she didn't notice the

girl's fork sitting right on the table where her plate was to go.

In one swift motion, Olivia had lowered the plate directly onto the fork. It skittered off on a horrible, unpredictable trajectory.

Oh, dear, Olivia thought. *This won't end well.*

It was as though time unraveled in slow motion: The plate skipped like a rock across a pond; the girl shrieked and bent backward in her seat. Impatiently, her maybe-father leaped to his feet, unfortunately catching the underside of the table as he did so.

Olivia wasn't sure what, ultimately, was to blame for the events that followed. It could have been the girl's shriek, which set her father off. It could have been the father rising as abruptly as he did. It could have been the simple unfortunate fact of a misplaced fork.

But regardless of the catalyst, the situation had all but blown up in her face. Olivia watched with horror as it happened, her feet glued to the floor. No amount of split-second reacting could have averted this crisis.

The table tipped over, spilling water on the three patrons and across the floor. The three plates hit the floor with a chorus of clinking and thudding. And the hummus landed directly in the young girl's lap.

Facedown.

"Ewwwww!!!" she shrieked, popping to her feet like a jack-in-the box. The plate slid off of her lap and

shattered noisily on the floor. She glared at her father, whose patience had clearly been stretched to its breaking point. "I don't even *like* hummus! It's just because *she's* a vegetarian!" She stared murderously at the pinch-faced woman, who resolutely refused to meet the girl's gaze.

Olivia's mouth dropped open. She had no idea what to do. None whatsoever. She looked down and saw the girl's pants smeared with chickpea paste, plus an array of chipped porcelain dotting the floor. The spilled water had made its way along the floor, and now other patrons were standing, fussing and fretting and stepping hastily out of the way of the mini tidal wave.

> *I was just getting the order to table thirteen.*

"*What* are you doing? Why are you just standing there?" Ingrid asked, nearly seething, she was so angry.

Olivia swallowed. "I was just getting the order to table thirteen."

chapter thirteen

"So you just left them all there, standing in a pile of soggy hummus and broken dishes? *Ai, mami,* that's a problem," Alexa said, sighing. She was leaning against the edge of Olivia's cubicle desk, her weight shifted onto her forearms. The girls were back at the *Flirt* offices, and the order of the day was gruntwork. Olivia was filing, while Alexa was archiving old photos. Poor Mel was off somewhere transcribing interviews, and Kiyoko was inputting the celebrity "Spotteds" for Trey. Rather, Alexa was *supposed* to be archiving old photos. But when she'd come across a hysterical portrait of Karl Lagerfeld and Josephine Bishop smoking cigars in Ibiza, she'd come running.

Olivia would have appreciated the picture, too—if only she hadn't been half-asleep at the time.

Kiyoko and Eli had been dead serious when they'd respectively warned Liv to wear flats to wait tables, she knew, but she hadn't read the more meaningful message behind their

"So you just left them all there, standing in a pile of soggy hummus and broken dishes?"

words: Waiting tables was right hard work. She was bone tired. The soles of her feet, her spine, her lower back all ached with a raging insistence. Thank goodness sequined Chinese slippers were acceptable footwear in the office. Even having worn trainers to work last night, her blisters had blisters of their own.

"She had a feeling that today was not going to be her day for divine inspiration."

She felt completely drained. Her eyes were scratchy, and her tongue was fuzzy. And meanwhile, she still had to prove herself to Demetria. So far, she'd not come up with anything spectacular on the "Haute and Heavy" front, and time was running out. Somehow, though, she had a feeling that today was not going to be her day for divine inspiration. She rubbed at her temples resignedly. "No," Liv answered Alexa, shaking her head glumly. "I helped to clean it up."

"And the family? What did they do?"

"They left," Olivia admitted. "Without paying their bill—understandably, of course."

"And what did Miguel say?" Alexa asked.

"He was quite nice about it, actually. I thought he'd sack me on the spot, but at least he's got a bit of a sense of humor. He asked the busboys to help me clean up, and he let me off early. Told me his first night had been hard, as well."

"So you've still got your job?"

"I've still got my job," Olivia confirmed. She yawned loudly, taking care to cover her mouth with her hand. Her manicure was completely ruined, she noticed. "Though I've no idea how I'll make it through another night. Not to mention, that waitress, Ingrid, just hates me."

"Maybe she's jealous," Alexa suggested.

Olivia laughed. "Of what? My complete and utter inability to succeed at a job that hundreds of thousands of people do every single day? Not bloody likely." She folded her arms on the desk and collapsed her head into them. "It's hopeless. *I'm* hopeless. I can't do it. I just can't manage an internship *and* a proper job—but if I quit, I'll have to go home. I don't have nearly enough money left in my bank account to last me through the next three weeks. I was supposed to use my cards." She looked at Alexa. "I suppose I sound dreadfully spoiled, don't I?" she asked ruefully.

Alexa waved her hand dismissively. "You do not have to worry about what I think of you. But that attitude, *chica,* it will never work out for you," she admonished. "And also, you should sit up." She poked Olivia in the shoulder.

Olivia straightened right up. "Awfully good friend

you are, poking me while I'm literally down," she said. She smiled halfheartedly to show that she still had some sense of humor about this all.

Alexa jerked her head to the side. Olivia whipped around in her chair—thank goodness it had wheels, after all, as she wasn't in much of a state for whipping around today—and saw Delia, Bishop's acutely tense assistant, striding down the hall toward them. Her Manolos clattered purposefully against the floor, striking a sonorous contrast to the swishing sound of her sleek pencil skirt. "Of *course* we have those for you," she was saying. "I'll just talk to the Photography intern. Andrea!" she called out, pointing a pen in the girls' direction. "Tatyana wants to see the outtakes from last week's shoot. Can you get them?"

Alexa nodded dutifully. "They're in the flat files. I'll run to get them."

"*Alexa,*" Tatyana said, smiling with recognition. She brought up the rear, her sparkly DKNY flip-flops and

❝ She brought up the rear, her sparkly DKNY flip-flops and velour Lacoste tube dress a sharp but playful contrast to Delia's *Blade Runner* meets *Office Space* interpretation of fashion. ❞

velour Lacoste tube dress a sharp but playful contrast to Delia's *Blade Runner* meets *Office Space* interpretation of fashion. "So good to see you again."

"You too," Alexa gushed, clearly awestruck at the model's ability to be continuously gracious and friendly. "I'll be right back with the shots. You will think they are *muy bonita,* I can promise you!" She scampered off.

"Olivia," Tatyana said, turning toward Liv's cubicle. She lowered her voice. "Did your friend get home okay the other night?" She looked one part concerned, one part teasing, which was okay with Liv.

"She did," Liv said. "But not without incident. We were caught by a photographer."

"I hate it when that happens," Tatyana said sympathetically. "They can be like wolves sometimes!"

Olivia laughed appreciatively. "I reckon it happens to you quite a bit more than it happens to me, so I'll have to take your word for it."

Suddenly, Tatyana's mouth formed a small *O* of surprise. She reached out and, before Olivia knew what was going on, firmly grabbed Liv by the chin. "*Where* did you get these earrings?" she gasped.

Olivia blushed. "Actually, I made them." She touched her ears self-consciously. They were small drop-crystals, very understated.

"No! They're incredible. I thought your beadwork was a hobby. I didn't know you were an *artist*."

Olivia shrugged. "Not really an artist. But I love clothes, you know, and I adore accessorizing. I think that because most of the time my own style is so quiet, I like to have a little bit of fun, express myself in small ways. I make all kinds of jewelry." She stopped, realizing that she was babbling. Tatyana certainly didn't want to hear Liv's whole life story!

But to Olivia's surprise, the model was beaming at her with obvious admiration. "I think that's incredible," she said. "I could never do something like that. Before I was a model, I could hardly dress myself!" she confessed.

Olivia giggled. "You're not the first model to say that," she said. "Though I have quite a hard time believing it."

"Believe what you will," Tatyana said breezily. "But you must let me borrow those."

> **Believe what you will, but you must let me borrow those.**

"Borrow them?" Olivia repeated, feeling like a parrot. Was she kidding? Tatyana was a *supermodel,* after all! Olivia would gladly give the woman the clothes off of her back. Though that could be embarrassing.

Tatyana nodded. "Yes, I have a shoot tomorrow for *Style* magazine. I've seen pictures of the dress—it's long and sheer, very dramatic. I think those earrings would be perfect." She winked. "Much better than letting the stylist choose. Much more personal."

Olivia could scarcely contain her excitement. "You want to wear my earrings in *Style* magazine? Goodness, of course." She pushed her chair back and jumped to her feet, practically clawing at her earlobes to hand the jewelry over to Tatyana. Once they were off, she dropped them into the model's cupped palm.

"I can get you a bag," Liv said. "So they don't get lost." They kept loads of ziplocks in all shapes and sizes in the fashion supply closet, for tagging and organizing all sorts of accessories. If Tatyana was interested in Liv's earrings, then Liv *certainly* wasn't going to risk the chance that they'd end up floating around the bottom of someone's Birkin bag!

"*Olivia,* what could you possibly be bothering Tatyana about? I'm sure she's rather busy and has places to be." It was Demetria, stalking down the hall like an anorexic cruise director. Today she was neogoth with her hair spiked with black streaks, arms adorned with henna tattoos, and a nose ring that Liv was reasonably sure was a glue-on, twinkling on the outside of her right nostril. Demetria looked decidedly displeased to discover a conversation taking place between her intern and her most in-demand model.

"Bothering me? Of course not," Tatyana insisted,

> **"*Yes, well, designing jewelry and designing couture are very different, of course.*"**

laughing. "I was the one who was harassing her, about these gorgeous earrings that she apparently designed. Did you know you had such a talent in your midst?"

Demetria drew her mouth into a thin line. "We all do just adore Olivia's work," she said, her teeth clenched tightly enough to break wood. "She's going places, I always say." She sounded as though she meant just exactly the opposite.

"Well, I'm going to wear these earrings at a shoot tomorrow, and I will make sure that the editors send you a tear sheet. We'll mail it directly to Bishop so she can see for herself who her next great designer may be."

"Yes, well, designing jewelry and designing couture are very different, of course," Demetria said, her fists curled up into tight little balls. Every muscle in her body looked coiled and poised to spring. "Olivia's just now learning about high fashion."

Tatyana rolled her eyes. "High fashion. Outside of the shows, who wears it? Not real women. Real women want to know how you can make high fashion accessible. That's what I hear when I do public appearances over and over again. Or they want that one amazing piece, and then they mix it with something really low-end, something that makes a statement. No one wants to be matchy-matchy fancy anymore. Besides," she finished, "sometimes you just want to, how do you say, 'keep it real'?" She reached into her glorious alligator-skin bag and fished out a pink-and-green plastic tube of mascara. Olivia recognized it as a favorite of Tatyana's in the "under-ten-dollars" category, which they had talked about in the restroom of the face-cream party. "You'll never convince me to switch to the expensive brands," Tatyana said.

"Keeping it real . . ." Olivia mused, more to herself than anyone else.

"Yes, well . . ." Demetria sputtered, obviously flustered and none too pleased about it. "Olivia is certainly a rising star."

Had Olivia heard her so-called mentor singing her praises so effusively before, she might very well have laughed aloud. As it was, however, Liv **"*Olivia is certainly a rising star.*"** was far too preoccupied to even notice. She'd been hit with the germ of an idea, the sort that could absolutely take off and develop a life of its own.

What a surprise.

Perhaps today is to be a day of divine inspiration, after all.

From: liv_b-c@flirt.com
To: flyguy@hh.net
Subject: My sidebar

By George, I think I've got it!

. . . .

From: flyguy@hh.net
To: liv_b-c@flirt.com
Subject: Re: My sidebar

Well, obviously. I never doubted you for a second.

chapter fourteen

Not surprisingly, the Friday night rush at Moe's was even more punishing than Thursday's had been. The slight advantage of this being Olivia's second actual day of work, rather than her first, turned out to be not very much of an advantage at all. She knew, now, which tables were which, and she knew how to load the orders up on a tray in such a way that she'd be more likely to actually distribute them to the proper patrons, but that was really it. Well, that and the fact that over the past four hours, she had miraculously managed not to douse any of the customers in organic food.

"Jeez, it's never gonna thin out here, is it? Everyone in New York wants to eat cheap vegetarian tonight." It was Eve, another waitress who was, thankfully, significantly more helpful and outgoing than Ingrid had been. Eve was a slightly pudgy redhead with a fabulous smile. Olivia had no doubt that she took in loads of tips, as she was warm and friendly and the customers clearly adored her. The good news was that the waitstaff pooled their tips together at the end of the night, which meant that Eve's good humor truly benefited everyone. The bad news was that as the restaurant's weakest link, Olivia deeply suspected that she was bringing down the average nightly take-home money of her fellow employees. But there wasn't much to be done about it other than to plug away. Surely she'd get the hang of this sooner or later, right?

Surely.

"It is right busy," Olivia agreed. "But I suppose that's normal, at the weekend?"

"I guess so. But that doesn't mean I have to like it." Eve stuck her tongue out. "My boyfriend's out with his buddies tonight, and I promised I'd meet up with him after I was cut. But, that's, like, never gonna happen. Even if it slows down, Miguel's going to have me marrying ketchup bottles all night long."

Marrying ketchup bottles? Liv wondered if that was slang for something. Something she'd been taught, that she was meant to know. She didn't have time to ask, though, as she saw the angular hipster at table five scanning the room for her. She dashed over. "Can I get

❝ The bad news was that as the restaurant's weakest link, Olivia deeply suspected that she was bringing down the average nightly take-home money of her fellow employees. ❞

you anything else?" she asked daintily.

He shook his head no, his sideburns a blur of motion. "Just the check, thanks. Right?" His geek-chic friend in Buddy Holly glasses nodded in agreement.

"I'll be right back with that," Liv promised as she headed off to write it up for them. She ducked into the break room, which was little more than a dingy closet but a haven from the throngs of demanding people. She'd had no idea how . . . *hungry* New Yorkers were. In just forty-eight hours, she'd developed a completely newfound appreciation for the service industry. In point of fact, she wanted to send them all on a week's paid holiday. But her tips certainly wouldn't cover that, regardless of how "on" Eve was tonight.

Liv heard the faucet run briefly in the tiny employee restroom. A moment later, Miguel emerged, whistling. "Oh," he said, upon noting Olivia sitting at the table. "I was looking for you."

Her heart sank. That could only mean that she'd done something wrong, that he needed to correct her or give her a stern lecture. How could she blame him? She didn't even understand the basics of waiting tables, like "marrying" the condiments.

"You were?" She forced a smiled onto her face. "Well, you've found me! Though, I've only been here for a moment," she amended hastily. She certainly didn't want him to think she'd been lounging behind the scenes all night while the other waitstaff worked their arses off. Too bad she didn't think she'd ever be able to stand again, much less rise and finish out the rest of her shift.

"I wanted to talk to you," he said.

Right, then. Here it comes, Olivia thought, bracing herself. *The riot act.* She was going to get fired, chucked, binned, pick-the-expression-that-you-fancy. Her fabulous foray into the working world had ended as quickly as it had begun. *Some good you are,* she thought. *Should have gone home when Mum suggested it. You might not have had your dignity, but at least, then, you wouldn't be so tired.*

"I know it's hectic out there . . ." he began, causing Olivia to stiffen even further until she was ramrod straight in her seat. "But you're doing a great job."

"I know," Olivia said, cutting him off and burying her face in her hands. "I've completely let you down, and I can't apologize enough." She paused, replaying his words in her mind. *A great job?*

"A great job?" she asked tentatively, her voice small.

He nodded. "Definitely. Of course, there have been some bumps in the road, but they're typical rookie mistakes you've been making."

"I dumped an entire meal onto someone's lap yesterday," she reminded Miguel helpfully, then

66 *I dumped an entire meal onto someone's lap yesterday.* 99

wondered if perhaps that wasn't exactly the best strategy to take in this situation.

"Trust me when I tell you that we've all done that at one time or another," he said, causing her eyes to widen with amusement. "The point is that you're friendly and you're a hard worker, and that's what counts. So I'm glad that you're here. I know the other waiters are, too. We were so swamped, and having someone else around—even someone who's not especially experienced—really helps. I hope you don't let a busy night like tonight discourage you from ever coming back, because we need you." He stopped, looking reflective, and then chuckled. "We *really* need you."

"But . . . I . . . well, okay," Olivia said, wisely choosing to quit while she was ahead. In a million years, she'd never imagined that Miguel would actually be singing her praises on her second night. But that didn't mean she was fool enough to stop him when he did. "I've got a lot to learn, I know," Olivia said, rising with her check in hand and getting ready to head back out to the floor. "But I will, I promise you that."

"I'm sure," Miguel said. "Kiyoko vouched for you, and she was right."

Olivia made a mental note to cut Kiyoko just that much more slack going forward. It was silly for there to be any tension between the two of them when obviously, they—how did Mel always say it?—"had each other's backs."

"And besides," Miguel continued, now grinning fiendishly, "our clientele would flip if we let you go. The customers dig your accent."

ⓖ   ⓖ   ⓖ   ⓖ

"Rise and shine!"

Liv carefully peeled open one eyelid, thoroughly disoriented. "What?" she asked, to no one in particular.

"Babe, lad, woman of the ages, it's—gasp!—eleven thirty A.M. Or, as some of us who are of the British variety might call it, half-eleven."

Olivia reluctantly opened her other eye as well to see Kiyoko staring down at her, fully dressed, in a garish Pucci-print knockoff skirt and sky-high platform slides. "Technically, Kiyoko, you aren't British, per se," Liv reminded the girl.

"Well, okay, 'of the globe-trotting variety,'" Kiyoko amended. "Either way, do you or do you not recall telling me just before you went to bed last night—and yes, you're welcome that I was actually awake, and at home at eleven on a Friday night, out of character but whatev—that you were meeting Eli for brunch and then a movie?"

Olivia propped herself up against her pillows. "That does sound fairly familiar," she admitted. She ran her hand through her short blond hair.

"Because it's the truth, lad! Anyhoo, I promised you I would get you up no matter how exhausted you appeared to be. Which, it must be said, clearly equals: extremely very. So go. Now. Or you will be late."

"So go. Now. Or you will be late."

Olivia couldn't decide if she was relieved or irritated that she had invoked Kiyoko into her plan. One the one hand, she was so tired, it felt as though there were tiny sandbags attached to the insides of her eyelids. On the other hand, in an hour she'd be having a chat and a laugh with Eli. So, it was a draw.

Who was she kidding? It was Eli, all the way. She'd drink five liters of cappuccino if need be.

She grabbed her shower things and blearily made her way out of the room. "I can't believe that you were actually awake before I was on a Saturday morning," she mused as she and Kiyoko walked down the hall together.

"You and me both, babe," Kiyoko agreed. "But I had an uncharacteristically quiet night in."

"Did I happen to—"

"—Stingy Lulu's, Avenue B."

"Right, then."

☾ ☾ ☾ ☾

"I can't believe you didn't know what biscuits were," Eli said, his eyes twinkling. "Were you raised by wolves?"

Olivia shrugged noncommittally. One of the good things about taking the waitressing job around the same time that she met Eli was that she was now able to be "normal" with him, or to go incognito, as it were. Eli was the first boy she'd ever dated who had known her as simply *Olivia,* rather than Olivia Bourne-Cecil. It was a very liberating thought, to know that someone appreciated you for who you were. All this time she had wondered what he would think when he found out who she "really" was, and now that looked like a reality she wouldn't have to face for at least another short while. A tiny voice in the back of her head suggested that this was, perhaps, flawed logic at best, but she pushed it out of her head, at least for the time being.

"*All this time she had wondered what he would think when he found out who she "really" was.*"

"In England, biscuits are cookies," Liv explained. "There'd be no reason to eat them with gravy."

"But you can see the benefits of doing it up, Uncle Sam style, right?"

"Now I can," she agreed. "You've opened up an entire new world to me."

They held hands over the remains of their early afternoon feast: the controversial biscuits and slabs of bacon that were far punier than what Olivia was used to. She'd come to discover during her time in the States that what Americans called *ham* was actually closer to the British definition of bacon. Though it still wasn't quite exactly the same thing. She supposed it was a good thing; by the time she got back home again, she'd be broken of her cravings. Mum would be pleased about that.

Yes, there were some things she was going to have to just do without during her tenure stateside. She glanced across the table at Eli, who was polishing off his coffee. He caught her looking his way and winked easily. She smiled back. Clearly, it was more than worth the temporary sacrifice.

"You're staring at me like I have three heads," Eli said, interrupting her internal monologue.

"Completely unintentional," she lied. "I was just staring off into space. I'm knackered. *And* I still have to come up with something brilliant for my sidebar—

and soon. I've finally had an actual idea, but I'm too exhausted to really think it through. Perfect, wouldn't you say?"

"Yeah, waiting tables takes it out of you," Eli said. "I did it one summer, but it wasn't my thing. You know, I'm a sensitive artist—temperamental, not great at remembering small details, prone to going off into my head sometimes . . ."

"So what happened?" Olivia asked, curious.

"Oh, you know," he said sheepishly. "I got fired."

Olivia burst out laughing. It was such a silly little story, and the fact that Eli seemed so embarrassed by it made it all the more endearingly hilarious.

"Glad you find my pain to be such a source of hysteria," he said dryly.

She shook her head and made a massive show of pulling herself together. Fortunately, the check came just then, so the moment was broken. They both grabbed for it at the same time, brushing their fingertips together, which sent small chills down Olivia's spine.

"You know I need to be the male chauvinist pig," Eli said.

"But I've actually made quite a lot in tips, believe it or not," Olivia explained. "Last night was brilliant! And anyhow, we pool them. Which works out quite well for me. Hopefully the rest of the staff—the experienced

> ## 66 *It was clear he had no intention of backing down.* 99

folks, that is—aren't too resentful."

"Well, experienced or not, you worked hard for that cash," Eli protested. "You should let it burn a hole in your pocket at least for another day or two."

She arched an eyebrow at him, but it was clear he had no intention of backing down. After a beat, she suggested, "Well, why don't we do the modern thing and split it?"

He considered that for a moment. "I can live with that," he decided. "I do like a modern woman."

They settled the bill and left the restaurant, strolling down Avenue B toward Houston Street, which was where they were going to see a movie. They'd made it only a block or two when Olivia was blindsided by an unexpected vision in Burberry.

"*Olivia*! I cannot believe I am running into you *here,* of all places, after you completely blew me off for coffee the other day!" It was Phoebe Winters, the very picture of righteous indignation in ash-blond highlights.

Olivia started back. "Likewise," she stammered. "How are you?" She was completely unprepared for this encounter, and felt rather like a deer in the proverbial headlights. The polite thing to do, she knew, was to introduce Eli straightaway. Unfortunately, the last thing she wanted was for Eli to get up close and personal with Phoebe.

As always, manners prevailed. "Phoebe, this is Eli. Eli, this is Phoebe. Phoebe and I are friends from back home," she said, hoping against hope that Phoebe wouldn't choose to elaborate. Her carefully constructed house of cards would crumble in an instant if Phoebe let on that back home, the two of them were practically royalty.

"Lovely to meet you, Eli," Phoebe said, smiling prettily, if a tad insincerely. "I'm fine, you know. Just coming from a lovely French brunch at Danal. Oh!" she said as if just remembering something. "We're all going to high tea at the British Society House tomorrow. They do it every Sunday—haven't your parents told you about it? Everyone goes, the whole gang from Hampstead. You should come along."

High tea at the British Society House sounded brutally dull. Liv could scarcely keep herself awake for those sort of functions when she was in Hampstead, after all. Of course, saying no to Phoebe would be practically committing a mortal sin. Thank goodness she had a valid excuse this time. But, how to break the

> ❝ **High tea at the British Society House sounded brutally dull.** ❞

news to Phoebe, who would surely think Olivia *completely* daft for turning her back on British high society?

"I'm actually busy tomorrow morning," Liv said, hedging a bit. *Better to be vague,* she decided. Though this subterfuge was getting awkward—Eli would wonder why she was being cagey about having a job.

"Oh?" Phoebe said, clearly not satisfied with this explanation. Obviously, one wasn't "busy" when the invitation came directly from the right sort of person. How, then, was Liv to be honest with Phoebe? Especially since Eli was now beginning to take a newfound and pointed interest in this exchange? So much for her short-lived "normalcy."

> **So much for her short-lived "normalcy."**

"I'm working," Liv elaborated. She took a deep breath and decided to just go for it. "I'm a waitress. Just down the street, actually!"

"*Really,*" Phoebe said in the same tone she might have used if Olivia had told her she was raising a legion of chipmunk fighter pilots in her wardrobe. Her nose wrinkled, almost involuntarily. "I must say, I'm surprised. No wonder your parents were so . . . *worried* about you." She managed to infuse this comment with a healthy dose of mannered disdain.

"What did they—" Olivia began, thoroughly

outraged. She stopped herself, though, before she could ask too many questions. Frankly, if her parents were spreading gossip about her, she didn't want to know. She'd taken the job at Moe's specifically so that she could be more independent and worry less about what her parents thought of her. Allowing herself to go mental at the slightest gossipy comment would be completely counterproductive.

"Never mind," Liv finished lightly. "Anyway, I really can't talk just now, Phoebe. Eli and I"—she indicated Eli, who smiled affably in Phoebe's direction—"are going to see a film. The period piece set in Derbyshire, you know." Obviously, Phoebe knew of it; their friend's manor had been used as the film's location.

"Yes!" Phoebe smiled. "You'll love it. Though you will absolutely *die* when you see what they've done to Ellie Ledger's estate house. You'll hardly recognize it. Of course, it *was* due for a bit of a makeover, but I still think it was a bit tacky for her parents to allow Merchant and Ivory to film there." She shrugged as though she simply couldn't be bothered with any of it anymore. "Well, I don't want to keep you," she said. She kissed first Olivia, then Eli, on both cheeks good-bye. "Lovely to see you—and to meet you," she said to them both respectively. And then, in a whirl of subdued plaids, just as quickly as she'd arrived, she was gone.

Once the coast was clear, Eli looked over at Olivia,

who had the funny feeling that she had some explaining to do. Obviously, her days masquerading as "normal" were over.

Several expressions fought to reveal themselves across his lovely features. The predominant expression, confusion, ultimately won out. "Friend of yours?" he finally asked.

Olivia nodded, wondering to just what extent, exactly, the jig was up right now. Was it worth continuing the charade? Should she just come clean with him? There were considerable pros and cons to either tack.

Ultimately, she managed a small "sort of," and left it at that.

Eli looked pensive for a beat or two. Then he looked downright uncomfortable. "You know what? I, um, have a test Monday morning," he said, rather suddenly. "And I haven't studied at all."

Olivia had the sneaking suspicion that this actually wasn't true at all. He certainly hadn't mentioned any test during the entire course of the afternoon. But she couldn't quite call him out on the grounds of dishonesty right now, could she?

"So, I'm going to go," he said. He leaned forward and kissed her quickly, stiffly on the cheek.

"" Olivia had the funny feeling that she had some explaining to do. ""

> ❝ *She felt terrible. But there was nothing to be done right now.* ❞

She contemplated several things to say and ultimately discarded them all. He waved and retreated.

She felt terrible. But there was nothing to be done right now.

chapter fifteen

It was awful," Liv said, resting her hand in her chin. "He just dashed off. I'm sure he'll never want to see me again."

"Don't be silly, Liv. He likes you," Mel said. "You just have to talk to him, explain why you played it the way you did."

The two girls were gathered over steaming mugs of herbal tea in the kitchen of the *Flirt* loft. "Rose hips," Melanie had said, after Liv explained to her the terrible unfolding of the afternoon's events. "Soothing." They'd headed off for a not-so-brief debriefing. Lovely Mel—she was wonderfully supportive and didn't once make Olivia feel guilty for the pure, simple fact that Liv had, of course, been dishonest with Eli.

"Explain to him that I essentially lied about everything to do with my family, my background?" Olivia said, sighing. "It's hopeless."

"Okay, it's not, you know, an ideal situation," Mel admitted. "I'll give you that. But you wanted him to like you for

Okay, it's not, you know, an ideal situation.

you, ironically enough. Don't you think he has to respect that?"

Olivia shook her head. "I hope so," she said. "But right now I can't be sure of anything."

◉   ◉   ◉   ◉

The brunch crowd at Moe's had a decidedly different vibe about it than the evening patrons, Olivia decided. They were more laid-back, more prone to lazily lingering over their meals, and slowly sipped thirds and fourths of coffee. Not that she minded. As long as she was attentive to when the coffee needed refilling, the brunch crowd was an easy group. She couldn't believe that she felt that way, but she did. Two hours into her shift and she was wide awake, perky, and on top of her tables. She knew the specials by heart, and she hadn't spilled one thing. Yet. And miraculously, her feet weren't even aching one iota.

Never mind, she told herself, banishing the negative thinking from her mind. *You're not going to ache.*

She knew the main reason that she was enjoying this shift so much was because it had managed to take her mind off of the situation with Eli. But that was just fine with Olivia.

The door swung open and in walked her three

favorite temporary New Yorkers: Kiyoko, Mel, and Alexa. "Hello!" Liv cried enthusiastically. She did a quick sweep to be sure that her tables were relatively content for the moment, then ran to the front door to greet them. "What a lovely surprise. What are you doing here?"

"We were hoping to eat," Mel said. "I hear this place is, like, organic?"

Olivia nodded. "Quite right. Should be right up your alley. That's Bennett—" She pointed to a goateed NYU student in jeans and a T-shirt that had seen better days. Bennett smiled at them wanly, looking somewhat noncommittal if not outright unfriendly. Olivia remained completely unfazed. "He'll seat you. Ask for my section."

They did, and moments later, she dazzled them all by reciting the specials without once consulting the board. She ran off to place their orders, then reappeared with a complimentary tray of fresh-squeezed orange juice. "On the house," she said proudly.

"Wow, you're, like, a serious professional," Mel said, taking in Olivia's apron and her happy grin.

> **You're, like, a serious professional.**

"I certainly am. Though I'm not sure that Eli thinks so anymore," she admitted.

"Why? What happened?" Kiyoko asked, looking

quite genuinely concerned. Olivia hadn't had a chance to fill the rest of the girls in on what had happened, and thankfully Mel could be counted on to keep a secret.

"I was trying so hard to be 'normal' around him— he was so different than the other boys I'd dated. I really wanted him to get to know me without the backdrop of my family and all that," Liv said.

"Fair enough," Alexa offered.

"Yes, I thought so. But we ran into Phoebe Winters yesterday."

The girls groaned almost in unison. They knew how Olivia felt about Phoebe, though of course Liv tried to be polite about it.

Olivia nodded. "Anyway, suffice it to say, the cat is out of the bag."

"How did he react?" Alexa asked, her forehead crinkling sympathetically.

"You could tell he was quite surprised, though he tried rather sportingly to pretend that he wasn't," Olivia said.

"I understand you not wanting Eli to judge you based on your background, but it seems like he passed the test, right? With flying colors?" Mel said. "If you want to have a real relationship with him, you're going to have to come clean eventually, anyway."

"I know, you're right," Olivia said. She gnawed fretfully at her lower lip, then stopped herself when she realized how unappealing it was as a mannerism. "I'll call him later tonight," she resolved. "Sort this all out." *I hope.* She heard a chime from the kitchen window that she recognized as her own prompt.

"Ladies, I have to dash—table eight's order is up."

Kiyoko flashed her a winning grin. "Spoken like a pro, lad. Spoken like a pro."

      ☉   ☉   ☉   ☉

Unfortunately, Eli didn't answer his mobile when Olivia rang him that evening. She left him a message asking him to please give her a call back when he had a moment, hoping that she didn't sound unintentionally dire or grim. But by ten o'clock on Sunday evening, the glitch in the road (one couldn't exactly call it a fight, really) with Eli had to be placed on the back burner. She had more important concerns: Tomorrow was the day that she was due to present her sidebar concept to Ms. Bishop and Demetria. The thought was enough to drive her mad. She didn't know how she was going to sleep one wink tonight. She'd been in her pajamas for the past thirty minutes, lying in bed and staring blankly at the ceiling, thoughts running circles 'round her brain.

She was well aware of how fortunate she was to be the recipient of Ms. Bishop's grudging support.

> **"She was well aware of how fortunate she was to be the recipient of Ms. Bishop's grudging support."**

Most of the girls—and in fact, half the staff of *Flirt*, for that matter—were right terrified of her. Olivia had the advantage of connections working in her favor. But even in this case, those connections had come at a price: Demetria's rather barbed resentment. Demetria had shot down every sidebar suggestion she had thus far. Certainly, some of Liv's ideas were probably weaker than others, but some must have contained at least a seed of an idea. No doubt about it, Demetria felt threatened by Olivia's family relationship with Ms. Bishop.

And now, after all of the back and forth, the "bouncing ideas off of each other," and the utter rejection of every notion that had crossed Olivia's mind, she was being called to the carpet in front of Ms. Bishop *and* Demetria together.

Horrifying.

She sighed. Much as she wanted to be fresh for tomorrow, sleep wasn't going to come anytime soon. She kicked off her duvet and padded quietly down the hallway toward the kitchen. A glass of water wasn't a solution, but it was something to do.

She poured herself a glass from the tap—Eli had obviously had no small influence on her tastes, she was both pleased and surprised to realize—and turned to make her way back to her bedroom.

"Hey there."

She nearly jumped out of her skin, then felt like a right prat to realize that it was only Emma standing in the doorway of the kitchen. "Goodness," Liv said, trying to recover as smoothly as possible. "I didn't see you there."

Emma chuckled. "I didn't mean to sneak up on you," she said. "But you were quiet at dinner. I could tell you had something on your mind."

Olivia nodded. "I have to go before Ms. Bishop and Demetria tomorrow to present my idea for a sidebar. I'm nervous." She shrugged. "I suppose it's silly."

"Of course it's not silly," Emma said, softly encouraging. "It's your career. You take fashion—and *Flirt*—very seriously. I would only expect you to be anxious."

"True," Olivia said.

"You're going to be great," Emma said, looking sincere. "There's a reason you got this internship, remember?"

"My family's connections to Ms. Bishop," Olivia mumbled, more bitterly than she intended, giving voice

> **_At the bottom of it all, her desire to be seen as normal and separate from the trappings of her background was an aching need to be seen as whole even without any of that._**

to her true, deepest insecurity. At the bottom of it all, her desire to be seen as normal and separate from the trappings of her background was an aching need to be seen as whole even without any of that.

Emma looked startled. "Sweetheart, I can understand why you feel like you have something to prove, but keep in mind, I've known Jo for years. I know how high her standards are. Do you think you're the only candidate who had any sort of leg up? Ms. Bishop gets asked for personal favors all the time. From some of the most powerful people in the world. Intelligent, creative people. Trust me, Liv, you wouldn't be here if you didn't deserve to be. It's a real coup."

Relief and affection flooded Olivia's system. "Thanks so much," she replied, genuinely moved. "That was exactly what I needed to hear." She felt at least a fraction of the tension ebb from her body and, as if on cue, she erupted into a squeaky yawn.

Emma laughed. "Do you think you'll be able to get some sleep, after all?"

Olivia nodded. "I reckon." She quickly hugged Emma and then headed off to do just that.

chapter sixteen

Olivia tapped the toes of her Stuart Weitzman pumps impatiently against the carpeting just outside of Ms. Bishop's office. For today's review, she'd broken out her most tried-and-true office-casual ensemble: a gorgeous Diane von Furstenberg wrap dress in a subdued-but-eye-catching print and a coordinated—but not *too* terribly coordinated—Coach satchel. The satchel, of course, was hardly necessary for an interoffice meeting, but she did love the way it looked against her dress. For good luck, she'd tucked a shimmery bobby pin that she had embellished herself into her hair.

Unfortunately, the most professionally polished, well-coordinated outfit she owned was doing nothing to quell her raging nerves.

> **The satchel, of course, was hardly necessary for an interoffice meeting, but she did love the way it looked against her dress.**

She glanced at her watch again anxiously. Half-eleven. She had been called in to see Ms. Bishop fifteen minutes ago and had been standing outside the partially closed door ever since. She could hear murmured whispers through the opening and was dying to know what Ms. Bishop could possibly be discussing with Demetria. Hopefully not Liv, or her subpar performance. Though, with Demetria, Liv couldn't be sure.

"Seriously? I am *so* completely and totally convinced that the fat-free yogurt down the street is, um, *not* fat-free at all. And—you can go in now."

"Pardon?" Liv started backward, realizing after an awkward beat that Ms. Bishop's rather chilly assistant, Delia, had in fact taken a break from her phone conversation to usher Liv into the CEO's office.

Right, then. Showtime.

Olivia forced one foot forward, then the other, willing her limbs not to tremble. This was Ms. Bishop, after all, who'd attended her coming out-party and her parents' silver anniversary. This reaction she was having was hysterical and more than a little bit unwarranted.

"Hello," she said, somewhat uncertainly, stepping into the office. Ms. Bishop sat perched at the very end of her chair behind her massive, yet utterly sterile desk. Demetria, Olivia was pleased to note, sat in one of the two chairs directly in front of Ms. Bishop's desk, and Ms. Bishop's computer monitor had been tilted outward.

The screen showed a spread from last month's issue that Olivia assumed they had to be going over. Which meant their conversation had had absolutely nothing to do with Liv. She sighed.

See, silly? Daft—and paranoid, as well.

"Olivia," Ms. Bishop said, peering at her from over a striking pair of cat-eyed glasses that Olivia recognized as Oliver People's fall collection. "Please sit."

Dutifully, Olivia took her seat. She cleared her throat nervously, unsure of what was to happen next. Funny how all of her brilliant social breeding seemed to fly out the window when her own passion was actually at stake.

> **Which meant their conversation had had absolutely nothing to do with Liv.**

"So, we wanted to discuss your ideas for your sidebar, for my 'Haute and Heavy' spread," Demetria began. "What can we do to make couture more appealing to our average reader, someone who doesn't necessarily have the body—or the income—of a supermodel?"

Olivia bit her tongue and resisted the urge to point out that "Haute and Heavy" had, of course, been her own idea. If there was a time or a place to correct one's boss in front of her own boss, this wasn't it. Unfortunately.

> **"** *If there was a time or a place to correct one's boss in front of her own boss, this wasn't it.* **"**

Ms. Bishop jumped in. "Yes, of course. What people don't always realize is that while *Flirt* has positioned itself as the foremost international fashion magazine in circulation, it has household recognition among almost all women, not just those who are familiar with high fashion. So it's important that we cater to them in order to maintain as much widespread relevance and influence as possible."

Olivia couldn't have asked for a better lead-in. *Here goes nothing,* she thought. "That was exactly my thought," she said, hoping that the quaver in her voice wasn't obvious to anyone other than herself. "For ages, it seems couture has been the domain of high society, and is looked upon almost as mere fun. But I'd love for it to be more accessible without actually detracting from its mystique and uniqueness. So I'd propose a spread that mixes the wildest of fashion with reliable—and affordable—mainstays."

Demetria's expression was unreadable. Ms. Bishop, however, seemed quite curious. Which was as it should be. "Can you give me some examples?" she asked, tapping her pencil against the surface of her desk.

"Certainly," Olivia said primly. She couldn't help but notice that her voice was no longer shaking—and neither were her hands or legs. "It came to me when Tatyana Milova was showing me the lip balm and the mascara that she uses. They're both from the chemist—dead cheap. And this from a woman who's worn earrings worth more than a car in some photo shoots. So that'd be the way I would go—mix high-end pieces with wearable, relaxed basics. A simple white tank under an elaborate velvet blazer. Levi's jeans and Prada trainers. A Hermès bag with"—she faltered slightly, feeling slightly self-conscious—"handmade jewelry. Playful, personal, and expressive."

> **66 Liv couldn't read her face to save her own life. 99**

Ms. Bishop's gaze flickered over Olivia's bobby pin, but she didn't say anything. Liv couldn't read her face to save her own life.

Demetria, however, had an opinion. "You are aware that almost every magazine does something like this at least once a year, are you not? How will we differentiate ourselves from them?" Her eyes were tiny, narrow slits that bore down onto Olivia.

Olivia steeled herself to press onward. "Of course, I had considered that," she said as politely and deferentially as she possibly could. "Firstly, I must say that the fact that it appears in so many magazines so regularly suggests that there is an ongoing interest in the topic. So there's no reason to shy away from the subject matter. As far as setting ourselves apart, I think that we can use our signature editorial style—fun, fresh, and flirty. I had a mind to run a sidebar of a contrast in extremes, for instance, the cheapest cup of coffee versus the most expensive that a person could possibly buy in New York City. Or the most expensive meal, or cheapest pair of sunglasses. And we'd run brand names and actual prices. The companies would welcome the publicity, and readers love that 'tell all' type of material. I'd love to write something like that."

For a moment, no one said a word. Olivia briefly considered running from the room in hysterics, and prayed silently to herself that the earth would actually open up and swallow her whole. What if Ms. Bishop hated her suggestion? What if Demetria never warmed to her? What if they fired her? Surely, if they fired her, she'd have to go back home, waitressing job or no. She'd have to face the whole crowd back at Hampstead. The people she'd spent all summer trying to set herself apart from.

She'd have to lose Eli.

That simply wouldn't do at all.

If she got kicked out of the program, she'd just

> **"That simply wouldn't do at all."**

spend the rest of her three weeks living in Mel's closet. Or under Alexa's bed. They wouldn't mind. They could sneak her food, and she could pay them a percentage of her tips—which had to pick up sooner or later. Or she could eat at the restaurant, provided she could muster up some enthusiasm for ambiguously designated "organic" fare. She could . . .

Her hysteria subsided as she noticed Ms. Bishop nodding her head in quiet affirmation. "Perfect, Olivia," she said, softly but definitively. "That's perfect." Her gaze traveled once more to Olivia's hair pin. "Tatyana mentioned that she was going to be wearing Bourne-Cecil original earrings for her *Style* shoot. I think that's fantastic. We should find a way to feature some of your creations in your sidebar, as well. You wouldn't mind that, would you?"

Mind? Is she kidding? "Mind? Honestly, Ms. Bishop, that'd be brilliant."

"No, dear," Ms. Bishop said, and this time she did allow herself a glimmer of a smile. "In this particular case, *you're* brilliant."

ⓖ   ⓖ   ⓖ   ⓖ

66 *She was far too excited to eat proper food just now.* 99

"So, is Demetria, like, breathing fire?" Kiyoko asked, grinning wildly and taking a healthy bite of her hot dog.

The interns had gathered for their usual lunch, blowing off the cafeteria for sunshine and street vendors. Olivia picked the salt off of her pretzel. She was far too excited to eat proper food just now. "Dunno," she said, shrugging. "Right about now, I don't much care, I must say."

"I don't blame you," Mel said, leaning over and impulsively enveloping Olivia in a hug. "But I'm not surprised."

"Of course not," Alexa chimed in enthusiastically. "And *mira, chica*, if the *Flirt* or *Style* stylists like your accessories—which, how could they not?—you could get more publicity than you can handle."

"I know," Olivia said. She sighed contentedly. "It's perfect." She smiled. "I feel like I've taken such a load off. Now I'm far too excited to get back to work. And Demetria has me on filing duty again."

The others groaned. "What are you going to do, then?" Mel asked.

"Oh," Olivia said coyly, "I have a phone call to make."

ᕒ   ᕒ   ᕒ   ᕒ

After the girls had finished eating, Olivia wandered off by herself for a chance to make her phone call in relative private—that was to say, with as much privacy as a New York City street corner afforded anyone. She punched in the transatlantic code, and after a moment or two of fuzzy beeping, her mother's voice trilled across the wire, coated in static.

"Hello, dear, is that you?"

"Yes, Mother, I've got some news," Olivia said, crossing her fingers to herself and hoping against hope that her mother would be as excited with this information as she was.

"You've decided to come home."

"Not quite, actually. But better than that, even. Ms. Bishop loved my idea for a sidebar and she's going to run it in the magazine!"

A hiss of static, and her mother's voice came streaming through the line again. "Well, that *is* lovely, dear," she said. Olivia decided she'd ignore the relative surprise in her mother's tone. "Which issue will that be?"

"September or October, depending on how quickly we can get the shoot and the copy done," Olivia said. "And . . . better yet, they're going to feature some of my own accessory designs in the spread, as well."

"That's just brilliant!" her mother said. Olivia could tell that she truly meant it, as well. "Father is away just at the moment—a meeting in Brussels, you know—but I'll be sure to ring him with the news straightaway. I'm so proud of you, dear."

Olivia's throat caught for a moment, quite unexpectedly. She was proud of herself, as well.

> **She was proud of herself, as well.**

"I meant to tell you, also, that I ran into Phoebe Winters's mother just the other day. She said that you saw Phoebe in—is it Alphabet City, darling?"

"Yes," Olivia said, dreading what was to come next.

"According to Phoebe, you've got a job as a . . . waitress?"

"Yes, that's true, Mother," Olivia confirmed. "Believe it or not."

"Well, dear, I have to say I respect your work ethic. But now that you'll be doing this spread for Josephine, you can hardly be expected to keep a steady job."

"Actually, Mum, I quite like the job," Olivia said. "And I'm getting better at it. Even my manager has said so."

"Well, that's smashing, really, darling, but I can't see as how you are going to be able to juggle a job as

> **Her independence had been so hard to come by that she was quite reluctant to give it up now.**

well as an internship. Truly."

Her mother had a point, Olivia knew, but her independence had been so hard to come by that she was quite reluctant to give it up now. Not to mention, she did still need the money to cover her living expenses.

As if scripted, her mother went on. "Of course, we'd be happy to reinstate your credit cards. You'll need some funding if you're to finish out your capacity as Ms. Bishop's protégé!"

"Well . . ." Olivia hedged, hesitant.

"Don't be proud dear, you know you could use the money," her mother said.

Olivia considered her options for a moment. "I reckon I have a compromise," she said. "How about I cut back my hours at the restaurant to be sure that they don't interfere with my work at *Flirt*? And maybe you can reinstate just one of the cards." She held her breath, wondering what her mother would say.

"I think that sounds perfect."

Brilliant! Olivia jumped up and down in place and tried not to outright squeal with excitement.

"One last thing, Liv," her mother said.

Olivia bristled, suspicious. Her mother absolutely *never* called her Liv. "Pardon?"

"I have a young man that I'd like you to meet when you come home."

Olivia exhaled slowly. "Perhaps," she said. "Perhaps. I'm still seeing Eli, you know. We'll have to see where that goes."

The two or three moments of silence that followed were the longest of Olivia's life. Had she pushed her mother too far? She couldn't breathe. She didn't know what she'd do if her mum took back her side of the bargain.

"Fair enough, Olivia."

"It's okay, Mum, I had a feeling—wait, what?"

"Don't say *what*, dear. Say *pardon*."

"Pardon?"

"Well, you've proven to me that your instincts can clearly be trusted."

"Really?"

"Really."

At that, Olivia's throat caught again. But only in the best possible way.

◉   ◉   ◉   ◉

"A compromise, huh? Sort of like me getting the rocky road and you getting the birthday cake bonanza and us switching flavors halfway through?" Eli teased, scooping up a bite of ice cream and passing it over to Olivia.

After she'd spoken to her mother, she'd tried Eli again on his mobile, hoping that she wasn't crossing the fine line from pursuer to stalker. Fortunately, he'd answered on the first ring and explained that his phone had died the night before, and he'd only just recharged it. She'd invited him to meet up after work, telling him that she had lots of good news, and they'd arranged to meet for gelato in Little Italy. Now they sat on a bench in Washington Square Park, Olivia's head resting lightly on Eli's shoulder as they traded spoonfuls and people-watched the afternoon away.

"Exactly. I'll cut back my hours, she'll give me some of the financial support that I had before, and I'll have time and energy left over for my internship. It's perfect. Or, almost perfect," she said, straightening up and looking at Eli directly in his piercing brown eyes. "It would have been perfect if I hadn't been hiding from you who, exactly, I really am."

"I'm not angry," Eli began, slowly and deliberately enough that Olivia knew there was more to come. "But

> ## It would have been perfect if I hadn't been hiding from you who, exactly, I really am.

> **66 *I wanted to be like you. And I wanted you to like me.* 99**

I don't understand why you thought you had to keep your family a secret from me."

"Where I come from, back in London," Olivia explained, "who I am is defined by my family. And when I met you, you were nothing like the boys I know from back home. None of them are creative, interesting, or introspective. I wanted to be like you. And I wanted you to like me. For different reasons than people back home do."

"Olivia, I like you because you're funny, smart, and sweet, not because you have friends or family in high places," Eli said.

"As long as you like me, full stop," Olivia said shyly.

"What do you think?" Eli said, reaching over and giving her shoulder a squeeze.

"I think I'm quite glad that I have three more weeks in New York with you," she said.

And she was.